SHERRY**ASHWORTH**

Sherry Ashworth was born in London. She started writing in 1989, and now has a total of eight adult novels and three young adult novels under her belt, including *Disconnected*, her first book for Collins. In a recent interview with amazon.co.uk, she lists Charles Dickens, Charlotte Brontë and Bill Bryson among her favourite authors. She now lives in Manchester with her husband and two teenage daughters. All of her books are set partly or wholly in Manchester, because, as she says, "of its vibrant working-class culture, its varied ethnic communities, and also because I know it so well."

DISCONNECTED

SHERRY**ASHWORTH**

Collins flamingo

An imprint of HarperCollins*Publishers*

Thanks to Andy McCullough of The Children's Society and the 1999/2001 sixth form at Bury Grammar School (Girls), all of whom provided me with vital insights.

First published in Great Britain by Collins Flamingo 2002

3 5 7 9 8 6 4

Collins Flamingo is an imprint of HarperCollins*Publishers* Ltd,
77-85 Fulham Palace Road, Hammersmith, London W6 8JB

The HarperCollins website address is www.**fire**and**water**.com

Text copyright © Sherry Ashworth 2002

ISBN 0 00 712045-1

The author asserts the moral right to be identified as the author of the work.

Printed and bound in England by Clays Ltd, St Ives plc

For Avril Bruten

It's hard to know where to begin, or how to describe what happened to me. I'm not even sure who I want to talk to. Or what I want to say. But maybe if I try to put all the different parts together it will make some sort of sense to me. So here's my story, and it's for each of you to whom I owe an explanation.

But, remember, I'm not sorry.

To Mrs Dawes, my English Teacher

Thinking of you makes me want to write down what I have to say. Do you remember the advice you used to give us when we wrote essays? Spend a long time on the introduction, as it's the first thing that gets read. Never answer the question in the first sentence. Make it clear what you're writing about by restating the question in your own words. You taught me how to be analytical. So here goes.

The question is, why did I throw away everything I had and end up as I am now? And as for the answer, I'm not even sure I know myself, but writing it might help me work it out. And it begins with me.

Me. Catherine Margaret Holmes. 16. Did well at GCSE. A good girl, nice family. Sensible. Prefect material. I remember how you used to smile at me encouragingly in lessons and say, "Well done, Cathy!" I used to hate that because I could feel everyone's eyes on me, and I just knew they were thinking, *teacher's pet*. I knew you liked me because of the way you nodded when I spoke and used to write those glowing reports for my parents. I liked you too because you liked me and even though the other students in the class teased you for those baggy cardigans you used to wear and the cup of strong coffee you used to take with you everywhere, I never joined in. Well, I did a bit, because you have to, really.

What I liked about you most was the way you got all lit up when you were talking about Shakespeare or poetry. You read things that none of us understood with your voice trembling with passion, then looked at us with your eyes shining, and we thought you were crazy. I can remember twitching with embarrassment for you but liking the way you were getting turned on. I tried to learn those lines you read...

Not poppy, nor mandragora,
Nor all the drowsy syrups of the world,
Shall ever medicine thee to that sweet sleep
Which thou owed'st yesterday.

You were saying, listen to the *sound* of the words, the pattern of the stresses – man*drag*ora, you said, lengthening the middle syllable as far as it would go. Man*drag*ora. Drowsy syrups. I thought of the cough linctus my mother used to give me when I was small, but I knew that was wrong, only you get these weird associations sometime. You told us how darkly beautiful these lines were, but the truth was, I didn't understand them, they didn't make sense to me. The effect they had was to unhitch me from the reality of the classroom and make me dream.

It was a small seminar room on the third floor where we had our lessons, grey plastic chairs around a scored wooden table. It overlooked tennis courts fringed with ragged trees. We were grouped around the table, one or two boys, and the girls, each one of them set and determined in their own way to get whatever it was they wanted. They scared me. Lucy had her head down scribbling notes as if her life depended on it; Melissa sat there weighing up everything you said as if she could strike you down at any moment. She had her hand over her mouth. Fliss and Toni sat together as perfectly groomed as air hostesses. I don't remember the others.

What I do remember from that day – the day I think it all began – was the sense of unreality that crept into the classroom. Like an animal, it rubbed itself against my feet and entered me, and I felt myself become detached and able to see very, very clearly, as if I was the only person in the universe, the only person who counted. I had X-ray vision. I saw behind your eyes as you were explaining the text that you were tired, harassed and anxious to get home. That Melissa was all spite and venom, glittering like a snake. That Lucy never had an original thought in her head and she was supposed to be my best friend. That Fliss and Toni were entirely plastic and even though they boasted about pulling blokes, they were so fake they wouldn't have felt a thing.

These were nasty thoughts, and I didn't like myself for being so bitchy. Does that surprise you, that I have such a bitchy side? It's not the real me. But nor is the nice girl that you know who obeys the rules and smiles at all the teachers. Nor is the Cath who flirts with boys and samples their kisses. Or my parents' daughter – she's not real either. Just for one moment my eyes drifted to the text of the play we were reading and I thought, here are a bunch of characters, but where is Shakespeare? And me too – I was just a bunch of characters – does this make sense? Or will you write in the margin, *avoid colloquialism, say precisely what you mean.*

What I mean was at that point reality receded for me and I wasn't really sure whether I was alive at all. My breath caught in my throat and I shivered. A prickling all along my veins made me want to run out of the classroom there and then but that was crazy – what would people think – and how could I explain? Was I having a panic attack? I'd heard people use that label before but I didn't know what you were supposed to feel if you had one. I tried to calm myself down by biting the sides of my fingers – they're red and raw, even now, like eczema. Bit by bit I went back to normal. My breathing regularised, my heart began to beat more slowly and I came back to the present and even felt slightly giggly.

But then real panic set in. I hadn't heard a word you'd said and I knew you were setting us an essay on that part of that play. Of course I could always photocopy Lucy's notes but the truth was they never made sense to me. I would have to work it all out by myself. There was nothing to be learnt now because Melissa had taken over. She was telling you that her parents had taken her to see the opera, *Otello*. You said that was wonderful!, and asked her about it. She criticised the tenor and talked about the set, pushing her hair back as she talked. The boys made faces and grinned at me which made me feel a whole lot better.

I want to know, did you ever see through Melissa? That was what really got us. That the teachers thought she was wonderful because she walked like you and talked like you and got high grades, effortlessly. Your approval of her shone out of every orifice. But the truth was, she despised you all, all the teachers. She got everyone believing that Miss Bradwell was a lesbian and no one was to go in to the changing rooms with her alone. She brought poppers into school one day and gave one to Afsheen without telling her what it was. Her mother did her GCSE coursework. Her father's a consultant surgeon and took her to his old college in Oxford to meet some professor or other and she said it was all arranged, she'd be offered a place there next year.

Sorry – I'm going off the subject. I can imagine you annotating this with the brown-inked pen you used for marking our essays – stick to the point, Cathy, *don't waffle*. I can tell you now I never did know when I was waffling. Everything I wrote seemed relevant to me, just like Melissa is relevant to my story too. Only perhaps she's in the wrong order. So back to me. Sorry about the meandering.

I was really worried about the essay you set. It was partly because I'd been drifting in the lesson, and partly – or mainly – because of all the other stuff I had to do. There was a History essay hanging over me which had to be in on Monday. There was a test in Economics. You wanted us to read *Frankenstein* for our coursework. I had my oboe practice. I'd promised to come back to school that evening to serve coffee at the parents' evening. And the Geography lesson was next and he always set us loads of things. I'd been invited to a party too, and knew if I went to that I'd be tired all Sunday. And I was so tired now. I guessed that was why I felt so odd in your lesson. Are you like that? The more you think about the work you have to do, the more tired you feel? I get a dragging sensation in my arms and the beginnings of a headache. That's one of my worst points, getting tired when I shouldn't. No one else seems as tired as me.

Will that do as an introduction?

To my mother

I walked home from the bus enjoying the open air and the quietness. I know you like our neighbourhood because it's so peaceful. You told us you need to be able to come home and relax totally, and with your job it's not surprising. Dad likes the house because it has such a big, mature garden, which is unusual for a modern housing estate. You liked the fact the house was new and a bungalow because it was less housework. I was glad when we moved here eight years ago as I had friends in the area and so it seemed an OK place to live.

I left Windermere Crescent where there was just the occasional car – no pedestrians – and then turned into Wasdale Close, where we live. There was no one about. I don't know why Dad thinks the garage door needs painting because it looks fine to me, but as you say, it'll keep him happy. I could tell by the closed look in the windows and the silence of the house that you were still at the surgery. That was OK. I quite like having the house to myself.

I unlocked the door, both the Yale and the Chubb

lock, and stepped inside, flinging down my bag, scooping up the letters and hoping, stupidly I know, that there might be something for me. There was one for Dr & Mrs Holmes which I knew would make you mad. It should have been addressed to Dr & Mr Holmes. You're the doctor. As I hung my jacket over the banister and made my way to the kitchen for some coffee I was feeling kind of weird, as if I was acting in my own life. Perhaps it was because the house was empty, and there was no one around to remind me I was real.

I grabbed some coffee and opened the biscuit tin, but it was empty. Naïve of me, I know. You think it's important that I eat healthily. You're proud that I've always eaten three regular meals a day. Snacking is a bad habit, and undereating is another danger for teenagers. You like proper, family, sit-down meals. I have told you we're one of only a handful of families I know who still do that, but you shrug and your eyes go all hard and defiant. I love you, and admire the way you fought to get where you are.

I knew that really I should get on with some work but I just couldn't face it, so I went into the living room and turned on TV. There was a cheesy chat show with people saying gross things. It was easy to watch and made me feel kind of smug, kind of better than them, all those people who didn't know how to lead their lives. You say these American chat shows are like freak shows, and you disapprove of them. You give me grief for watching them. So it's just as well you weren't in.

I sprawled on the settee and it was nice, just letting everything go. I decided to shut my eyes and just listen to the shouting and abuse on the screen. The next thing I knew I heard your voice.

"Catherine? Are you asleep?"

I was, but I came round pretty quickly.

"No. I just had my eyes shut."

"Good, because if you sleep now you won't be able to sleep tonight. How was school?"

"OK."

"Did Mrs Dawes give you your poetry essay back?"

"No. I don't think she's marked them."

You tutted and carried on chatting as you rifled through the letters. "Typical. These teachers, they expect you to hand work in on time but they can't be bothered to hand it back. It sends out the wrong messages. And I wanted to know what she thought of it as I'm certain it's better than the last. I can see English Literature might be a weak link as the results in the English Department weren't all that good last year. Dr and Mrs Holmes! I just do not believe it. It's the twenty-first century and everyone still assumes a doctor is a man. How was your Economics – are you finding it any easier?"

"It's all right."

"All right? What do you mean, all right?"

"All right." I pouted at you. You didn't seem to see that I was tired and wanted to forget about school.

"Because it's important that you understand each new concept thoroughly. You have to build firm foundations. I can remember having trouble with Physics when I was in the sixth form because of some poor teaching in the fifth form. That was what decided Daddy and I to send you to St William's. Choosing the right school matters a lot. And I don't regret our decision. Every penny we've paid in fees has been worth it. Not that I'm saying you couldn't have got those GCSE grades by yourself. Your ASs should be just as straightforward. Of course, it's not just that *I'd* like you to get good grades, but I know that *you'd* be disappointed with anything less than the best."

Yeah, right.

"You're a perfectionist, Catherine, just like me. I'm all in. They added on five emergency appointments to my schedule – at least I'm not on call tonight. Time to catch up with the BMJ, I daresay. Daddy said he might not come home till late – there's something happening at the golf club. I'll take one of my lasagnes out of the freezer. When are you starting work?"

Maybe you said all that, maybe you didn't. I don't listen to you all the time. I think you talk just for the sake of talking. It's not that you like the sound of your own voice, but everybody has to bear witness to you. I don't mind, really. I'm used to it. I know you were a little disappointed I didn't want to be a doctor but you said a barrister would be just as good. Or a company secretary. I didn't argue because I trust you. You know better than me about careers and stuff, and anyway, me going to work seems a long way off. It even seems crazy to me that I'm in the sixth form!

"When are you starting work?" you asked me again.

"Later," I said.

"What do you mean by later? Before dinner, or after dinner? I need to know."

I felt a flash of irritation.

"I don't know. I might not do any work tonight."

"Why? Are you going out?"

"No. I'll just chill."

I saw you bridle and shoot me an odd kind of look – as if you were worried and scared of me, both.

"Chill? What kind of English is that? Are you hot or something? Honestly, it's as bad as that silly expression 'cool', which I never liked. And Catherine, you can't – as you so elegantly put it – *chill*. You are taking four A-levels. Four demanding A-levels."

I said nothing. That way I could stay in control. You paused, sizing up the situation.

"You'll feel different after dinner, I daresay."

You went over to the drinks cabinet and poured yourself a gin and tonic. Gordon's gin, and Schweppes Slimline Tonic. You drank every evening and because it was so regular it seemed normal and acceptable to me.

"Can I have one?" I asked you. You swung round, looking guilty and alarmed.

"Don't be silly. You don't have to copy my bad habits." The joke was meant to defuse the situation.

I refused to smile. I was as taut as a bow, watching you, as if I was seeing you for the first time. You didn't care much about your appearance, you never did. You always laughed when I put on some make-up as if it was a childish, or worse, a rather common thing to do. Your hair was short but almost deliberately dishevelled – clever women didn't have time to fuss with their hair. That day I remember you wore a grey skirt and a black sweater that screamed Marks & Spencer. You thought you looked classic, timeless, but I could see the little lines that radiated from your lips like cracks on an old oil painting. I observed the tiredness in your eyes. I felt sorry for you and glad I was young. But at the same time, or following on from that, I felt angry at you because you were my mother, which was just so claustrophobic. I didn't know how to judge myself without using your eyes, your tired, ageing eyes.

When I'm with my friends, I never talk about you. We don't talk about our parents unless they're being a pain. It's good to escape. But then I come home and it's like living in your shadow – and that's good, because in some ways you make me feel safe, but in other ways, I want to scream. Is that normal? You're the doctor. You should know. And I hate it that I think you know everything about me. You never worried when I was ill, and you tell me, all the time, that I'm just going through a developmental stage.

But I don't want to be like you because your life is so drab and monochrome and hard and you're so tired all the time. Like me. I'm tired all the time too.

I thought, I just can't be arsed to move. Not that I'd ever say that to you.

We had dinner that evening at the breakfast bar in the kitchen. We just small-talked – well, you did, going on about the bank statement and redecorating the porch and hallway, and whingeing about your paperwork. I refused dessert. You said you wished you had my willpower. Then you said, "Are you going up to your room to work now?" It was a challenge.

"I might," I said.

Two pugilists, eyeing each other from their respective corners.

"And there's your oboe."

I hated my oboe just then. She had pulled it over to her side.

"Because, Catherine, I know it's hard sometimes to get motivated but the secret of academic success is persistence and determination. It's always the student who keeps going who gets there in the end. I'm only telling you this for your own good. Really, it's nothing to me whether you work or not."

I was silent.

"Well?" she asked.

I took refuge in ambiguity. I got up, said nothing, and went up to my room.

It was a relief to be alone. I love you, but sometimes there's too much of you. Once in my room, I threw myself on the bed, wondering what was wrong with me that night. I worked out I wasn't pre-menstrual, but I didn't believe in that crap anyway. Girls I knew just said they were pre-menstrual so they could have an excuse for having a go at people, or a big cry and all their mates would cuddle them. I didn't feel like crying but just like things were out of joint. Worse, as if nothing mattered any more. The idea of not doing any work was so appealing. Like, what was the point?

But automatically I opened my schoolbag and took out my History text books and file, the document question he'd given us and an A4 pad of paper, and got myself organised. For a moment or two I actually felt like working. I like the look of a piece of blank paper. But as soon as I wrote my name, that same lethargy descended. It was such an effort to write. I tried to read the documents but they made no sense. I glanced at the first question – *Explain briefly the following references: (a) 'patrons and nominees' (b) 'the absurd admiration of the triumph of physical strength in France'.*

I felt paralysed by the weight of the words. A sensible

voice in my head (yours?) said, come on, now! It's only a short question. You can do it. Another voice said, what has this got to do with you, or with anything for that matter? It's all a silly game, taking exams, getting qualifications. It doesn't matter, any of it.

Only, if it doesn't matter, what does? That was what scared me. So I tried again. I began a sentence of my own on the paper in response, but then was distracted by the reflection of me in my dressing-table mirror.

Girl at work. Or girl not at work. My brown hair was dishevelled since I'd taken out my hair bobble. The expression on my face was blank. I automatically asked the mirror the question I always did – am I good-looking? This time the reply came back – what does it matter? In reality I suppose my face changes depending on my mood. When I smile I look quite pretty – my eyes are large, which helps. But at other times my face is heavy and formless.

So I got up to put some music on to help me start work. You have this rule, I know, that I'm only allowed classical music to work to – you read somewhere it aids concentration. Today I decided to go against you because I wanted to listen to a tape Greg, a boy in my Economics group, had lent me – The Smiths. From the Eighties. But they weren't like what I thought of as Eighties at all, but camp and suicidal all at once. They were good. I lay on my bed and listened and thought, I could get into this.

A shame I didn't like Greg that much, at least not in *that* way.

Then I decided to give myself a manicure. It can be quite therapeutic, doing things with your nails, or plucking your eyebrows, self-grooming. And I needed to get myself looking good for Brad's party on Saturday. I was half-listening for you because I didn't want to be discovered not working. But who was I kidding? I felt as guilty as hell. The more I put off working, the more I felt squeezed by some sort of invisible pressure. I couldn't breathe. But I couldn't work either. I thought about re-jigging my work schedule and doing double tomorrow. That seemed like a good idea. Or I could wake at six in the morning and work then.

I heard you shouting up at me.

"Catherine? Are you busy?"

"Yes," I replied. "Very."

"OK," you said.

I got my headphones out of my cupboard and put them on and carried on listening to The Smiths.

To Taz

You know most of this, but I'll tell you again.

Lucy texted me to say she was outside in her parents' car, and if I was ready, they'd give me a lift to Brad's party. She could have rung on the doorbell but Lucy would text in preference to talking sometimes. I shouted goodbye to my parents and confirmed I'd be back by one. A wonderful moment as I left the house, closed the front door, heard the lock click into place – cool, dark air, and the promise of a night in which something might actually happen. But only a moment. As I climbed into Lucy's parents' car the radio was babbling and Lucy's mother was babbling and Lucy herself kept up a whispered monologue about Brad whose party it was and who would be there and was her fringe OK? And her lipstick? And what about her nails? The polish came free with a magazine. And so on. I knew she went on like that because she was nervous. She'd only ever almost had a boyfriend, and that bothered her. For Lucy, going to a party was like buying a lottery ticket; this time, it might just be her. If her nails were right and her hair was right.

Brad's house was quite near us – about ten minutes away. It was an ordinary-looking semi-detached house, with a multi-coloured pane of glass in the front door. Lucy linked with me as we walked up the curved front path and rang the doorbell. A friend of Brad's opened the door to us and I watched Lucy straining to see who else was there.

Everyone was in a large room that extended from the front of the house to the back garden. Against the windows at the back was a large table with newspaper over it and cans of beer, bottles of Bud Light, and some Bacardi Breezers. There was also a huge mixing bowl full of crisps. The music was pretty loud – some repetitive dance music. But when I looked around the room I also saw a badly-painted portrait of Brad and his family with silly grins plastered on their faces and his mum looking impossibly young and pretty, and framed photos of some old people and a baby. And there was a sideboard full of glasses, that heavy crystal cut glass, and decanters, and some pottery figures of shepherds and shepherdesses and little child-like animals with large eyes. And for some bizarre reason someone had thrown a blanket over the TV and video.

Lucy was still linked to me and I felt her grip tighten.

"Oh, God," she said. "I don't know anyone here. Brad said there would be more people from our Business Studies set but there aren't. Oh, Cathy, just look at *THAT*!

Isn't he gorgeous? Shall we have a drink? Shall we go and see what there is? Or shall we find the loo first? I'd like to check my hair. You look gorgeous, by the way."

Before I knew it she had dragged me out of the party and we were on our way up the stairs, past a turn with a little occasional table with a dull white vase holding dusty artificial flowers, and Lucy began to peer in each room.

"No, that's a bedroom, and that's a bedroom – it doesn't look as if his parents are in – and this must be Brad's bedroom. Oh, look, he's got that huge poster of Eminem. Ah, this must be the bathroom." Lucy switched on a light and I followed her in.

Immediately she began fussing in front of the mirror, twiddling with bits of hair. I leant against the wall and noticed the clutter by the side of the bath – a Marks & Spencer bubble bath, a body moisturiser, nail clippers, Calvin Klein aftershave, little coloured bottles of aromatherapy bubble baths, an underarm shaver, an off-white sliver of soap with small hairs attached – I averted my eyes and saw that by the side of the toilet was one of those knitted ladies sitting discreetly on top of a roll of toilet paper, hiding it with her skirt. It made me smile. Brad made out he was such a cool guy at school. Brad wasn't even his real name. He was Martin Bradley Cropper.

I didn't like the way I was seeing through everything that night. I took hold of myself and focused on Lucy.

Actually it was quite easy to get involved with her preoccupations, as they felt so important to her. I helped her put some wax on the strands of hair at the sides so they fell the way she wanted them to, and we put some glitter by the corner of her eyes. I knew Lucy was fussing because it put off the awful moment when she would have to go downstairs and face everyone. I kind of felt the same way as her, but for different reasons. Lucy was worried about what people would think of her; I was scared about what I might think of the other people.

Don't think I was trying to be clever, or that I was up myself. It didn't feel like that – but you know what I mean, Taz. The truth was, I wanted to be like Lucy, someone who really believed that Brad's party was going to be top, someone who liked everyone they met, who was warm and open and good company. But I just couldn't be that person. I felt more like a shadow with the ability to pass straight through people. Perhaps it was because I hadn't slept much the night before.

Eventually we did go downstairs. Fliss and Toni had arrived and they squealed when they saw us and Lucy squealed back and I forced my mouth into a smile. There was lots of whispered gossip, stuff about who was coming later, and who might fancy who. Fliss and Toni wore stiff new jeans with diamante beading down the side of the legs, and tiny sleeveless tops with high necks. They both wore their hair down and daringly, Fliss had a pink hair extension. I wondered whether Toni's had fallen off. If I'm honest, they made me feel dowdy. I'd pulled on my silvery-grey trousers, the ones that shimmer, and the dark grey T-shirt with the words *Go Slow* – you never gave it back to me, did you?

I stood with the girls and looked over to the drinks table where the guys had congregated. I knew most of them and had pulled one or two – it made me a little sick to think of it now. None of them was one hundred per cent fanciable; Brad was so tall he stooped, Matthew had bad skin, Chris had cheeks like a hamster. It wasn't that I dreamed of the Mr Perfects that you see on films and TV. In many ways they're worse. For a start, they're not real.

Brad came over to say hello to us with a stupid grin stretching his mouth.

"Why have you got a blanket over the TV, Brad?" Fliss asked.

"Yeah," added Toni.

"The old man insisted. In case anyone scratches it."

"Oh," said Toni.

"Oh," said Fliss.

"What's that in your hair?" Brad asked Fliss, fingering her extension.

"Leave it out!" Fliss giggled.

"He's terrible," Toni said.

"Have you got one?" Brad asked, messing Toni's hair. He was having a good time, and it made me smile.

I could sense Lucy restless by my side, feeling ignored.

"Shall we go and get a drink?" she said.

Melissa arrived while I was sipping at a Coke and Lucy was knocking back a Bacardi Breezer. She had a tall, blond boy in tow, with cold blue eyes. She gave the impression she was just dropping in, and looked around, giving everyone time to get an eyeful of her. She wore black hipsters that accentuated her flat stomach and a tiny kid's top with a cartoon character on it. It hugged her bust possessively. I watched people drift over to her as if they couldn't help it. Even I felt her pull. Simply not going over to say hi to Melissa was a statement. In the end I had no choice. Lucy dragged me over.

"Oh, hi Catherine, hi Lucy. You look nice."

Patronising bitch, I thought. But I just smiled.

"You look gorgeous," Lucy said. "I love your top! Where did you get it?"

But Melissa didn't hear her. Some guys had come over and she was flirting, properly flirting, you know, with her hands, touching people's arms, nuzzling up to them. It was clever, in a way, what she was doing. The boys were hooked. No one was actually listening to what she was saying; they were just waiting for the moment when she might make them feel special. It was like Lucy and I didn't exist. Which was OK by me, but I could feel Lucy sagging.

Brad appeared then, having abandoned Fliss and Toni.

"Have you got a ciggie?" Melissa asked him, stroking his arm.

Brad shook his head. "It's a bugger. The old man doesn't like smoking in the house. I'll open the garden door if you like and you can smoke outside, if you can find a fag."

"Don't bother," Melissa said.

Brad looked crestfallen. I saw him shoot a glance back to Fliss and Toni who were now being chatted up by two short boys I'd seen around school.

"Is that painting of you?" Lucy asked him.

His face lit up again. "Yeah, it's crap, isn't it?" he said, grinning again from ear to ear.

"No," she said. "I think it's lovely."

Time, I realised, to separate myself. I wandered off to the settee by the bay window, which was empty, and sat down to watch everyone.

I could see the party was beginning to take shape. Some of the girls were moving to the music and Melissa, as foul as she was, made the party seem important, somehow. Some guys were laughing and getting more plastered. It was noisier and noisier by the minute. I liked just being there. It was restful not to be me but just an onlooker, outside life.

Even the scenes earlier in the day seemed apart from me, as if they'd happened to somebody else. Mum's grand inquisition, *why haven't I seen you working? Is there something wrong, Catherine? Peter! Help me here – she's being so uncommunicative!* And locking myself in my room again and looking at my books and my bulging schoolbag like a malignant growth sprouting blackly in the corner. I recalled burrowing under my duvet, and sleeping. Then I went downstairs rubbing my eyes, and lied that maybe I was fighting a virus and it would help me to go out tonight. Mum said, *you silly girl!* but spoke the words affectionately. I returned upstairs, and soaked in the bath, considering my pale body that seemed to belong to someone else. Then there were pangs of guilt about my oboe practice – little lappings of panic – and I began to wonder why it was I hadn't done a stroke of work for days. It wasn't as if I'd made a decision not to work. Something outside me had made that decision, and then I found the reasons to back it up. Or maybe not. I didn't know. I didn't care. I relaxed, regretting the fact the water was cooling. Then I was back on automatic pilot, drying, dressing, applying some make-up, on my way to Brad's party. And here I was in his front room, disassociated, watching people.

You could tell people had had quite a bit to drink already. They were loud, fooling around. Some boys were dancing maniacally over by the sideboard and I could see Brad – who was still talking to Lucy – cast them anxious glances. Some girls I knew were screeching and eyeing the boys up, ready for an assault. Fliss and Toni were slow-dancing with those short lads, and their hands were everywhere. I could see the boys watching each other, comparing moves. Synchronised snogging. Melissa dancing suggestively with her escort.

Then someone put on an album of Beatles hits – and there was that old anthem, *All You Need Is Love*. The boys sang it aloud, putting their arms round each other's shoulders, as if they were at a football match, shouting out the words. Soon nearly everyone had joined them. You could see written on everyone's faces that they knew they were having a brilliant time. They were happy and drunk and proud and hot and sweaty. All you need is love. Brad had his arm round Lucy's waist. Lucy gesticulated to me to join them. I couldn't. I had to stay where I was. Had to.

Not that anyone cared. The song ended, the group broke up, Brad kissed Lucy, and Melissa plus escort moved past me towards the door.

"Sad, aren't they?" Melissa said.

Her escort just smiled.

"We'll move on," she said. The escort offered her a cigarette, which she accepted. She stood in the doorway as she took a few drags. Brad was now on an armchair with Lucy on his lap. I didn't want to look at what they were doing. Instead I watched Melissa. She looked disdainfully at her cigarette, then swiftly threw it on the carpet, and stubbed it out with the toe of her stiletto.

"Let's go," she said.

The little bubble of hatred I felt for her was the first real emotion I'd experienced in days. I wondered whether I ought to tell tales to Brad, or confront Melissa. Then the complexity of the situation, the knowledge that Melissa would deny everything, that the whole affair would mushroom out of control made me tired again. Weary. Not so that I wanted to go home, but that I just wanted to stay on the settee in limbo like this, indefinitely. I didn't want my life to move on. I was happy to be a shadow. Or maybe it was everyone else who were the shadows, and I was the only living person. Or maybe I was going mad. I was faintly disgusted, slightly jealous of all the bodies intertwined, glad to be different, but very lonely. I wanted to be like everybody else. I was getting a little sorry for myself. Worse still was the fact a boy was eyeing me up, a chubby, spotty little boy who obviously thought he was in luck. Each time I looked at him I could see him trying to smile.

And then there was a commotion at the front door. It pulled me out of myself.

"I don't know who you are. Hold on a minute. Brad!"

Brad didn't hear, for reasons that I told you.

"Sod off. This is a private party! Brad!"

Chris pushed through and disturbed Brad. "Some blokes, say they know you. Won't go away."

Then you appeared. You didn't look like a drunken, brawling gatecrasher at all, but you did look as if you were at the wrong party. For a start – you don't mind me saying this – you were the wrong colour. All of the crowd I knew was white. It wasn't that we excluded people who weren't, but the Asians we knew at school formed their own little clique, and they didn't socialise with us out of hours. So I noticed you for that reason. And the way you knotted your hair. And the dirty leather trousers. But most of all for the look on your face. Slightly defiant, a little ill at ease but totally self-contained. Your chin was lifted, you held yourself still, Taz, and you neither smiled nor frowned. The blokes who came with you did the talking.

"We're mates of Brad's brother Rick. From The Pit. I DJ with him."

I saw Brad hesitate. He explained to Chris that it was true; Rick did DJ at The Pit, and he might have seen one or two of these blokes before.

"Is Rick coming later?"

"Yeah. When he's finished work. We've brought some stuff."

Another of your crowd had a Threshers' bag with cans of Special Brew. That decided Brad. He moved aside and you all came in. Still, he kept an eye on you all, and was relieved when your mates sat on the floor and just drank quietly.

You didn't drink. You didn't sit down either, but were chewing, standing by the door that led to the kitchen.

Then Fliss and the boy she was with sat down beside me and carried on touching each other up. It made me feel sick. I stood up to give them more room and that was when our eyes met. You smiled at me, not flirting, but a smile of understanding. I smiled back. But something happened then – you know it did. We made a connection.

I forget how long it was before you came over to me. I knew you would. Together in silence we watched the party like it was on a screen. It was so noisy we couldn't talk much. You asked me what I was called, and I said, Catherine. Cat, you said. I liked that. Cat. A shadow in the night. Yeah, Cat. Who are you? I asked. Taz. I questioned that. I didn't say so, but I thought it sounded like one of those kids' chocolate bars. You said it was short for Tariq. Cat and Taz. It sounded good. I liked the way that being called Cat made me feel like someone new.

Then you cut through all the bullshit about school and college and exams and said, was I having a good time? Not particularly, I said. And you laughed, but more to yourself. You said you thought I looked fed up. You said, any reason? None at all, I said, but I am fed up. Totally.

Me too, you said.

We didn't have to say anything for ages after that. Then you asked me if I wanted a drink, and I said I didn't drink. You looked a bit surprised, but I saw you weren't drinking either. I smelt cigarette smoke on you, but that could have been because you'd come from a bar. Standing close to you I noticed the gold stud in your nose and I could see you were cracking the joints in your fingers.

I know what you're thinking. Did I fancy you then? The truth: I don't know because you were so different. I coveted your difference. I wanted to *be* you, with knotted hair and a pissed-off look and leather and piercings. I realised I'd had enough of being me and that was the trouble. I was worn out. Like a train out of fuel in the middle of a tunnel. Imagining being you was such a relief.

You asked me what music I was into. I blustered, talked about The Smiths, Tupac, Green Day. You mentioned some bands I'd never heard of and I felt small. One of them was Transponder. I remembered that afterwards. I asked if you hung around at The Pit, and you said, sometimes, if you had the dosh.

In between our snatched questions, I could see people stealing glances at you. Some were curious, some a little suspicious. When Lucy came up for air and saw me with you she grinned, thinking I was in luck too. I liked her then because I could tell she hadn't judged you. You were a bloke and that was good enough for her. But if I was you – and I wanted to be you, remember – I would have hated the way sneaky eyes labelled me as different and dangerous and somewhat disgusting. My crowd, you see, for all that they acted so cool, were just like their mums and dads: middle-class, conventional, into exam grades and good jobs and settling down one day. It was OK to be wild on Saturday night because that's what Saturday nights were for. But you had to be steady for the rest of the time.

Only it was Sunday morning now and for the first time in ages I felt totally awake. Every sense of mine was sharpened. I was living again. Someone shoved you by accident and you fell against me, but when you righted yourself you stayed close. Cat and Taz.

And then your mates re-appeared and said, come on, nothing doing here, and you cast me a regretful glance – see ya, you said, touched my hand, a rush of cold air as the front door opened, and you were gone.

To Mrs Dawes (2)

Was it a week later? Or two weeks? I forget, and it doesn't matter now. I had to see you to discuss my progress at school, or lack of it. It wasn't my choice. I hadn't asked you for help. The fact I had stopped working only made me panic occasionally. For the rest of the time I enjoyed feeling slightly mutinous. There was something brave about not working, a kind of passive resistance. Only none of my teachers saw it like that. I presume that was why we had to have the little talk.

You tried to make it as cosy for me as possible. You borrowed the deputy head's office and took her chair – with its extra cushion giving support for her bad back – and carried it round to the front of the desk, so you could sit close to me, but at an angle. So I knew you cared, but that you meant business.

First there was the small talk about the weather and the noise from the builders who were constructing a new Chemistry lab. I joined in but wished you'd get down to it for your own sake – seeing the uneasiness in your tired, puffy eyes.

"Well, Cathy," you said. "You know why I wanted to see you."

I decided to act along with you, feed you the lines you wanted to hear. It was easier that way, and besides, I didn't want to upset you. It wasn't your fault.

"Because I've got behind with all of my work," I said.

"Yes. Yes, that's right. Do you want to run through with me what you're owing?"

You didn't mean to, but you made my essays sound like deposits in a bank. Things that I *owed*. A debt to my teachers.

"Well, I'm late with an Othello essay, and I don't think my poetry assignment will be ready tomorrow. There's a couple of pieces of History, and one of Economics, and a Geography test I haven't revised for."

"This is not like you, Cathy."

That was such a weird thing to say. As if you knew the *real* me I wasn't being. But I didn't want to argue.

"No, it's not like me," I said.

Vertical blinds shading the window. A smear of polish along the ledge where the cleaner hadn't done her job properly. The distant sound of drilling. In-trays and out-trays full of files and folders and papers and a blotter spattered with coffee stains. My shoes, regulation black but with high platforms and frayed laces. Your shoes, flat Hush Puppies, distorted by the shape of your foot. Your black skirt just fringing your knees, which were pointed towards me. Your hands clutched tightly in your lap.

"Is there any problem, anything you want to talk about? As far as possible, I'll keep any confidence. And if I have to pass on what you say, I'll tell you first."

Standard school counselling stuff. I remained silent, playing for time. I debated whether to try to make something up. I could say I hadn't been feeling well, but the trouble with that was having a doctor for a mother. She'd know I was pretending. And even if I was ill, she wouldn't take me seriously. I could go on about some boy letting me down, or say I wasn't eating. If it were any other teacher, I probably would have. It can be fun to lie. But because it was you, and despite your pathetic fear of not conforming, I liked you. I had to try to hit at the truth, and see what you would make of it.

"I just can't seem to work at the moment."

"Is there a reason?"

"Not really. I just... There's so much of it."

"Believe it or not, Cathy," you said, laughing, "I know how you feel. I feel like that most evenings. But do you know what I do? I break it down. I don't let myself think, I have three sets of marking as well as lesson preparation and dinner to make and the boys to pick up from swimming and the examiners' reports to look through – I tell myself I can only do one thing at a time. One thing at a time. So I ask myself, what shall I do first? OK, I say, just the Year Eight stories. So I get those out and mark them. One thing accomplished. So I feel better already. And maybe I don't read the examiners' reports. And I'm learning not to beat myself up if I don't manage to complete everything, and instead to acknowledge what I have achieved."

Poor old Mrs Dawes, I thought. What a crap life.

"I know work can seem overwhelming at times," you went on. "But see if you can break it down."

You were repeating yourself now. Teachers always do. They're terrified you didn't quite get what they said, or you might forget it. Never mind about boring you rigid. I wondered what sort of people became teachers. Were they control freaks, or people whose own lives were such a mess that they tried to impose order on everybody else? Or kids who never really grew up and wanted to stay in school for ever? Or sadists? Our Maths teacher in primary school was a sadist. She *wanted* someone to get the work wrong so she could have the fun of punishing them. Sorry, Mrs Dawes, you weren't like that. You were one of those women who wanted to mother everybody, to care for us all. It was why I agreed to talk to you. I knew you didn't have it in for me.

"Cathy – would you like me to help you construct a timetable so you can catch up, and see your teachers so that they know you're working at it?"

No, I didn't. For a moment I hated you, loathed you. Felt you had gone over to the enemy. All through my life, people had been telling me what I had to do, giving me orders. Learn your spellings for a test, draw a picture with your story, do these sums, copy out these notes, then later, learn for your exams, and afterwards all that comparing marks and totting up averages and bitching. Then GCSEs and all those nameless, faceless people with power of life and death over you. And the sheer cheek of it, people asking you all these questions and making you jump through hoops so you could be like them.

Then you're in the sixth form, and they expect everything from you. History, Geography, English, Economics, and maybe, Catherine, you could keep on all four for your A2s. And the school orchestra – important for putting on your UCAS form. And remember to read round your subjects. And spend some time in the careers room so you have an idea what courses and universities appeal to you. Oxford or Cambridge maybe? The mad glint in your parents' eyes when the teacher mentions those two magic words at parents' meetings. Of course, there would be extra lessons, extra work, but Catherine can manage it. The Economics project. One whole day out at a History day school so I have to catch up on the poetry notes and I don't understand Seamus Heaney anyway. Or Gerard Manley Hopkins. Somebody translate, please. And the Geography teacher slagging us off. *You're lazy, the lot of you. The mid-year test will sort you out, show you how you've been sitting on your backsides.*

Oh, and I forgot. It's important to be a well-rounded sixth former too – you must do more than just work, otherwise you're boring. Read the papers, watch documentaries, get a job, help at school events, do some voluntary work, and work experience – that's vital. These days, when it's so much easier to do well at exams, work experience and your hobbies and interests count as never before. You need to pay more attention to your technique when you're answering questions in exams to get those few all-important extra marks. It can mean the difference between an A and a B! But make sure you have time off too. Take up yoga. Exercise. Listen to music. Read. Read lots. Here's a reading list, two reading lists, three.

"Cathy – you're not crying, are you? I'm so sorry – I'm not very good at these things. Here, have a tissue. It's OK to cry – look – you're starting me off! Come on, you've got so much going for you. Nobody's angry with you – I can promise you that."

You didn't realise they were tears of rage.

"I don't think I *want* to work any more," I said, testing you.

I could see you floundering. It was a terrifying thought to you, that someone could choose not to work. Work, work, work. It was the teachers' mantra. Hard work and moral virtue were interchangeable.

"I know how you feel. We all feel like that from time to time. I know I do. But stick in there, Cathy! Remind yourself how much you love what you're doing. And good A-level grades could open the door to *any* university!"

Your cheery tone didn't deceive me. You'd snapped the handcuffs tight. So I should start working in order to get the opportunity to work more. It all made perfect sense.

"English Literature is your first love, isn't it?"

I knew what you wanted me to say. I didn't have it in me to disappoint you.

"Yes, I suppose it is," I replied.

"Cathy, listen!" you said, bending forward intently so I didn't have the choice. "If literature is what you want to study, then you MUST. It's a myth that's there's no job at the end of it. There's advertising, business, law conversion, publishing – even teaching. Look – I'm going to suggest something really naughty, really unprofessional!"

I could hardly wait. The most unprofessional thing I had ever seen you do was end a lesson twenty seconds before the bell.

"Go home tonight and do nothing but your English. Do something you love and rediscover why you're studying in the first place. You're in the sixth form – you chose your AS-levels yourself, you're not following the National Curriculum any more."

You were breathless with excitement.

"OK," I said. Because I wanted to please you. I wanted to enter into the fantasy that I could go home and get turned on by Shakespeare and write and write and hand in an inspired essay. And if I believed I would, maybe I *would*. Maybe I'd just lost faith in myself. Your optimism boosted me like a dose of caffeine. I didn't want all your hard work to be wasted. I knew you'd given up a free period to talk to me, and that you'd have even more marking that night as a result. The least I could do was make you think your efforts had been worthwhile.

"Perhaps I need to prioritise a bit." I knew this was talking your language. I saw you smile.

"That's absolutely it, Cathy. I hardly know why you need me, you're so good at analysing your own problems. Prioritise. It's just to do with your time management. Sometimes very clever people find difficulty with the simpler skills. That's you all over."

And like an ebbing wave that rush of optimism left me. It was the words 'very clever' that did it – don't ask me why. They made my limbs ache.

"Just try the *Othello* tonight – or the poetry – either one will do. Even if you only spend half an hour. As long as you enjoy it. That's what counts. Otherwise, what's the point?"

So you *do* understand, I thought. There is no point, because I'm not sure I enjoy working any longer. The panic returned. And I gripped the base of the chair I was sitting on, and tried to breathe steadily and deeply. No good. I had to change the subject.

"So both your sons swim, then?" I asked. It was a lucky hit.

"Yes. Michael swims for the county – he's the butterfly champion. Only I do wish they'd call it something else. He's fourteen now and it doesn't sound very macho. The butterfly champion. Though when you watch him you can see the power that goes into that particular stroke. Once he almost dislocated his shoulder. You don't have any brothers, do you? But perhaps you have a boyfriend?"

"Not exactly," I said. And thought of Taz.

"You will," you said, with an inward smile. Then you asked shyly, "Has this little chat been helpful?"

"Oh yes," I said. "Very."

I could see you looked a whole lot better.

To Dave

The night the drinking started I was getting hassle from my mother. I don't mean she was shouting her head off or anything – it was worse than that. There was all this tension swimming around in the kitchen. She'd drop in an innocent-sounding question. *Did I have a nice day at school?* She meant, had anyone been speaking to me about why I was so behind. *Did anything happen today at school?* In other words, she actually knew Mrs Dawes had spoken to me – she was probably behind it – and she was letting me know that she knew. And then there were these awful silences. I could hear her chewing and swallowing her food. It made me feel sick. I couldn't eat while she was eating. *Have you finished your Economics assignment yet?*

I knew what would happen. She'd hold herself in until she couldn't stand it any more and then she would start. *You don't know how much your father and I are worried about you. You're throwing opportunity away, Catherine. If you tell us what's wrong we can help you.* And she sounds so reasonable and it makes me feel worse than ever. The only way I could see myself escaping a nightly lecture was if she was called out. I told you my mother's a GP – that was her night on call. I even found myself wishing someone would have a heart attack or something, then felt guilty, and hoped instead someone was having a baby suddenly. And believe it or not, the telephone rang, and there was some emergency.

Reluctantly Mum got her stuff together and asked me to load the dishwasher. Believe me, that wasn't a problem. I heard the door bang and her car engine start up. Peace at last.

Except it wasn't peace. The peace suffocated me like fog. Then I wondered again if I was suffering from depression. I knew about the various sorts because I skim-read newspapers and magazines. Clinical depression – that's the serious one you have to go to the doctor about. Manic depression – where you have mood swings. Mild depression – how everyone feels most of the time if they're honest. Chronic depression – but that wasn't me either. I could feel OK, sometimes. I wasn't working simply because I couldn't see the point any more. And also I wanted to see what would happen if I didn't work. Mrs Dawes – my English teacher and form tutor – she said I'd *chosen* to be a sixth former. Only I was beginning to see that wasn't true. There'd always been this pressure on me to do what everyone else expected. I reckoned the first real choice I was making was this one. I was choosing not to work.

Then I felt mean. I knew I was freaking everyone out, making them worry about me. That wasn't part of my plan. That afternoon I'd promised Mrs Dawes I'd try an essay, so I pulled in my school bag from the hall where I'd dumped it and put all my books and notes and files on the breakfast bar. That alone made me feel better. Just creating the appearance of work restored normality.

There was a lot to do before I actually started work. I had to find where I'd written the title of the essay. Then I had to find the place in the play. Then some blank paper. Then a biro or pencil from the bottom of my bag that hadn't run out of ink or had a broken lead. I felt like a kid again. I used to love sitting at my desk in my bedroom with my anglepoise lamp and my set of fifty Derwent colouring pencils and my Barbie pencil case and furry animals lined up watching me work, being a good girl, knowing Mum and Dad were downstairs, approving of me.

Still the atmosphere wasn't right. It was too quiet to work. I wondered about putting on the kitchen radio but the DJs annoyed me. I just wanted to listen to pure music. So on the spur of the moment I grabbed my books and pen and went into the lounge, put my things on the coffee table, and put on one of Dad's CDs of opera arias. Don't look like that, Dave. Opera isn't only for snobs and saddos. If you let it, it can really get to you – all that raw emotion. But I only ever listened to opera when I was alone.

So I tried to settle down again and felt OK. I was about to work. I wrote the title of the essay on a sheet of paper in order to concentrate fully.

Taz came into my mind then, a boy I met a couple of weeks previous, at a party. The other day I'd mentioned him to Brad, whose party it had been. He'd said he'd never seen him before in his life. Sometimes when I was on the bus going through town I looked for Taz, but I was out of luck. I knew if I was brave enough I could talk Lucy into going to The Pit with me, but that might be hard now she was unofficially going out with Brad. Unless Brad wanted to come along too. Sorry – I've lost the thread. I was explaining about the essay. It was supposed to be on the audience's response to Iago.

I went into HMV to look for some stuff by Transponder – the group Taz liked – but there was nothing. I was too shy to ask, just in case I'd heard him wrong. Maybe they were just a small band starting out. Hip-hop, probably. You can tell a lot about a person from the kind of music they like. I bet you like Oasis and Robbie Williams. So do I sometimes, but that night, like I said, I was listening to opera. *Tosca*, actually. Dead sophisticated, me. And so that was when the thought came into my mind, though it was more of a joke. What I need to complete the picture is a G & T. Yes – opera, Shakespeare and a G & T.

The essay was easy, really. Iago is the villain, sure, but

the way he lets us in on his plans makes us part of them, and we admire his cleverness. And his language. Mrs Dawes always likes us to go on about language. It's *how* it's said as much as what is said. Yeah, yeah, yeah.

There seemed to be little point in writing the essay seeing as though I could answer the question.

I thought I would try a gin and tonic after all.

I knew this wasn't like me. Up until that evening I thought people who drank regularly were rather sad. It seemed like a weakness – it was one of the things I despised my parents for. I'd noticed the way they both came back from work all tense and snappy, then as they worked their way through a bottle of wine they'd unwind, chat a while, crack some jokes and then act stupid and not realise it. So I decided never to drink.

But that night I thought, what the hell? I *deserve* a drink, all the hassle I've been getting.

Took a tumbler from the kitchen, opened the bottle of Gordon's, glugged it out and retched at the oily smell. Filled it to the brim with Slimline tonic, wrinkled my nose in disgust and knocked it back. I couldn't see what all the fuss was about, why people made such a big deal about drink. I took the tumbler back to the coffee table where my books were and tried to start the essay with my pad of A4 paper on my lap.

We first see Iago in Act One, scene one, on the stage with Roderigo, in the middle of a conversation which establishes the main action in the play so far – no, not *so far*, as it hadn't begun yet – ... *the main action in the play, which is that Roderigo has given him – Iago – money and promises...* I knocked back some more gin. I could feel it now making my legs go heavy but at the same time my head felt light, as if something had lifted, as if I'd woken up. I wrote on furiously. *And he's worried that he's been double-crossing him so Iago expounds* (good word, that! Mrs D will love it!) *his feelings for Othello. The audience can see right from the start of the play that Iago is jealous of Othello and also of Cassio, who has just been appointed...* More gin. It made my pen flow. I realised that all that had been wrong with me was that I had been worrying too much. Taking it all too seriously. Writing English essays was as easy as falling off a log backwards. Backwards? Was it backwards? It amazed me how well I knew the play. Even if I was telling the story and not answering the question it should be obvious that I was answering the question in a way. As long as I wrote something, it was better than nothing.

Jealousy is an interesting emotion. Was I jealous of Lucy? I don't mean because I fancied Brad – give me a break! – but because she had someone. Or was I jealous of Melissa? A harder question to answer. I thought I simply couldn't stand her, but the truth might be that I was jealous. I didn't like her but I wanted to *be* like her. Or maybe I was jealous that she didn't choose to hang around with me. So I resented her. I decided I was pretty mean, deep down. But then, so were most people. I thought I didn't know one truly decent person. Everyone has an agenda. No one does anything unless it benefits them.

That struck me as being very wise and very true. I looked down at the paper and saw I'd written three quarters of a side. A bit messy, but I did have the pad perched on my knee. My gin was finished now so I thought I'd have some more. The novelty of what I was doing was cheering me up.

How much to pour in the glass? Might as well be generous. Emptied the tonic into it. Took a gulp right there by the drinks table. I really didn't know what I had been worrying about. Anything was possible. My whole life was ahead of me. I waltzed over to the CD player in time to the music, and turned up the volume. This was cool. I went back to the essay, only I didn't feel like getting on with it at that moment. I knew I could finish it now. Tomorrow. I would finish it tomorrow. I would wake up early in the morning and write and write.

The only thing that was wrong now was that I was on my own. I felt good, better than I had for ages. I wanted to *be* somewhere, at a party, in a club, messing with my mates. This was a waste of good feelings, sitting here alone. I wondered about ringing Lucy, but the thought of her wittering on about Brad didn't turn me on. Then all of a sudden the opera struck me as being stupid, so I ran upstairs and got Green Day and put that on instead. You can't stand still to Green Day. So I started to dance – it made me thirsty – I drank some more. Out of my head, I thought, I'm out of my head. That was exactly where I wanted to be. Instead I was the music, at last I was connecting.

The funny thing when you get pissed is that a bit of your mind stays sober. It's like a little watchful gnome that gives you important information – mind the vase of flowers, watch the time. And though it wasn't late I knew Mum could be in at any moment depending on the severity of the emergency, and that I didn't want her to see me like this. The little gnome calculated that she might notice that some of the gin had vanished, and that I could probably get away with telling her I'd had some, provided I didn't seem too affected by it. From time to time she and Dad had positively *tried* to make me drink.

So I turned down the music and tidied up, though the whole thing struck me as terribly funny, Green Day and Shakespeare and me nicking Mum's gin and being drunk like this and I was so relieved that I could feel good again.

Luck was on my side. I was already undressed and ready for bed when I heard Mum come in. I dived into bed still feeling giggly. In a moment or two she was knocking on my bedroom door. I said she could come in.

She looked at me enquiringly so I told her I'd been working on my Othello essay and I saw her face lighten. I said I was tired and that I would finish it in the morning.

"You look happier, Catherine," she said.

I agreed, smiling at her. She smiled back, and went out.

Cool, I thought, and reached for my Walkman by the side of the bed. I put on the headphones and started listening to some hits album. When I shut my eyes I felt as if I was spinning out of sync to the music. Scary but nice.

And that was it. So like you can see, the first time I drank to get drunk it didn't hit me as a big revelation or anything. It wasn't like it changed my life. It was just that it made me happy. It brought me back to the world. And I knew I wouldn't get dependent on it like my parents; for me, booze would be a way of having fun. That's all. Just fun. I suppose it's the same with you. You look the sort of person who'd go down the boozer with his mates. Or maybe have a can or two of lager in front of the telly. So you can't blame me, can you?

To Taz (2)

The next time we met was on the steps of the old Rialto.

On Wednesdays I had a free afternoon. Free afternoons were a sixth form privilege and one which I was in danger of losing. They'd had this meeting about me in school and my mum had said that maybe they should make me stay in school and work. But the Head of Sixth and Mrs Dawes had said that might make matters worse. That's what my dad told me.

He'd sat me down a couple of evenings ago like we were at some sort of business meeting. *I just want to take a cool look at the facts,* he'd said. *We'll keep emotions out of it. You need to know that your mother and I are puzzled. Puzzled and angry. Puzzled and angry and upset too. The facts are that we're paying for your education, you're wasting the best years of your life. Christ! We've done everything we can for you! And this is the return you make!* His temples throbbed in rhythm to his words and made him look ridiculous. I wanted to laugh.

Forget about him. Luckily – very luckily – I still had my free afternoon. I didn't want to go home so I wandered into town to get an Easter egg for Lucy. The newsagents were full of them, Cadbury's and Nestlé and mountains of Creme Eggs and Creme Egg Easter eggs, and chocolate button Easter eggs, Smarties eggs, Easter bunnies, chocolate rabbits, masses of choice, so much choice I just couldn't choose. In the end I went for Galaxy.

Chocolate's not a big thing with me; I can take it or leave it. But the girls at school are silly about chocolate and make a big fuss about not eating it, or eating it, and some of the Christians have given it up for Lent. But then they'll have loads of Easter eggs once it's Easter. I reckon it's the way some people give their lives meaning. They deprive themselves of quite boring things so that when they can have them they seem exciting. But they're not, in actual fact. A bar of chocolate. Cocoa powder and loads of chemicals. Big deal.

So I got the egg and looked at the magazines in the newsagent's, then went to browse in Our Price. Nothing much there. Outside, a breezy day, blue sky, white clouds scudding about, bits of sunshine. I was in a blank mood, a state of absolute neutrality, not one thing or another. Just didn't want to go home. Didn't want to think of the prospect of the school holiday.

I thought I'd go to TK Maxx and look at the clothes. I had to pass by the old Rialto. Once it was a dance hall, they said, then it was a bingo hall – I think I remember that. Then the bingo hall shut down and someone tried to turn it into a club, but there was scandal about the bouncers and drugs. So it was boarded up again. But the problem was, it was a Grade II listed building so they couldn't knock it down. And in the afternoons the moshers hung out on the steps.

As I passed them I gave them a glance, and you were there.

My heart started thudding. I walked on, turned the corner, and stopped. I knew I should have gone over and talked to you. I mean, I knew you and everything. But over a month had gone by since Brad's party, and I wasn't sure if you'd remember me. And it was embarrassing, really, because I'd been thinking about you a lot – I wouldn't say I had a crush on you, exactly – but you'd kind of grown in my mind. But I was pretty sure you hadn't given me another thought. I was worried that if I talked to you I'd probably be dead self-conscious and give myself away.

Then I did that really stupid thing that girls do – and boys, probably. I decided to walk back and pass the steps again – slowly, hoping you'd notice me and make the first move.

So I turned, slung my bag with Lucy's Galaxy egg in it over my shoulder and passed the steps again. You were sitting down, your elbows on your knees, not talking to anyone. I looked at you and our eyes met. I could see you were trying to place me. I ventured a little smile. You frowned for a moment then your face lit in recognition. I walked up to you.

"It's Taz, isn't it?" That gave you time to remember me.

"Cat?"

I was so relieved.

"Yeah," I said. "From that party you crashed."

"What are you doing here?"

"Bunked off school early." That was a bit of a lie but it sounded right.

"You still at school?"

"Sixth form," I said.

By now your mates had noticed me and were looking in my direction. I felt awkward. I'd seen the moshers hanging round town lots of times but I'd never paid them much attention. I suppose if I was absolutely honest I looked down on them. I wasn't into heavy metal and thought all their rebellion was a pose – they all dressed exactly alike, for starters. Only now I was so close to them I saw they were individuals, like you. I remember Steve and his grey baggy pants, Mac's braided hair – they were both there that day – and Bex in that enormous parka that swamped her. They looked pale and tired, but close-up, not much different from me. Steve's hair was dyed a bright red round the edges. Mac had combats with chains on the side.

"Cat," you said to them, by way of introducing me.

They all said hi, quite friendly, not curious. I felt really straight and boring in the tailored trousers I had to wear for school and the grey coat my mother had got me from a department store.

"How've you been?" you asked me.

"Fine," I said. My parents thought I had problems, and so did school, but I didn't.

We chatted a while and I re-familiarised myself with you. You wore torn jeans, a baggy sweater two sizes too big and a blue streak in your hair that was spiked up. Your clothes were hard but your face was soft – I think that was because of your eyes. They had depth. I forget what we said to each other but there was still that weird feeling that we knew each other well. I just prayed we could keep the conversation going as long as possible. I didn't want to lose you again.

Then your mates got up and said they were going on to someone or other's place. You looked at them, then at me.

"Fancy a coffee?" you asked.

"Yeah, OK."

So we wandered off together. I was happy to go wherever you wanted and to my surprise we ended up in the covered market. It was a smelly old place because they had the fish and meat markets at one end. The stench was rank. You went over to a little snack bar where they sold burgers and suchlike as well as hot drinks.

I said a black coffee would be fine. You said you were hungry and you ordered yourself a ham sandwich.

That got me curious. Once we'd sat down at a little Formica table with little pots of salt and pepper and a plastic sauce bottle, I decided to ask you.

"I thought you didn't eat pig meat."

"I do," you said, and grinned. I was pleased I hadn't offended you.

"Aren't you religious, then?"

"It's all stupid."

I was pleased to hear you say that. It was what I'd been secretly thinking. All the people I knew at school who professed Christianity were some of the most judgmental, smug, hypocritical people I'd ever met. And God is only another version of Father Christmas, to me, at any rate. But I guessed it would be slightly different for you. I knew Asians were more into their religion. And that it was more of a family thing.

"Do your parents give you grief about eating pork?"

"Yeah, well, I'm not a proper Muslim, am I?" You seemed jumpy and cracked your knuckles. "My Mum was a Muslim, but she married my Dad who wasn't. So that was it as far as her family was concerned. She was a non-person."

I'd heard of that kind of thing happening and I was appalled. I tried to encourage you to tell me more but the coffee arrived.

"So were you brought up as any religion?"

"My mum tries to teach me stuff about Islam but she's wasting her breath. I'm just not into it."

I asked you what you were into. You told me you played bass guitar and were looking to be in a band. That you were at college and doing Media Studies and Art and Photography. That you wanted to do an art foundation course somewhere next year. That you worked some evenings in a petrol forecourt helping a mate of your dad's. That you were fed up with this crummy country and one day you were going to live in the States, New York, probably, or Chicago. It must have sounded like I was interviewing you or something.

Then you asked me about me. I didn't tell you much because I thought anything I'd say would put you off. Little Miss Boring, that was me. Still at school, living at home. And I reckoned you didn't want me pouring out my heart about how everyone was hassling me. I was perfectly happy sitting with you in the snack bar being Cat, drinking foul black coffee with its bitter aftertaste.

"Are you still hungry?" I asked you, once you'd finished your sandwich.

"I'm always hungry," you said.

"Hold on." I brought Lucy's egg out of my bag and began to unwrap it. I saw your eyes light up. I wanted some chocolate too, to take away the taste of the coffee.

I broke you off a huge fragment and you shoved it in your mouth the way boys do.

"Oy!" said the woman from behind the counter. "You can't eat that here!"

She was looking at you, although I was eating too.

"Sad old cow," I said.

"Bugger off, the pair of you!"

You were on your feet in an instant. I was cooler than you and collected my things together dead slow on purpose. I thought she didn't have any right to talk to me like that. In a few moments we were pushing our way through the market eating chocolate and laughing, dissing the woman in the snack bar. It sounds corny but being told off had brought us together. Not in a romantic sense, but we'd both been victims. We stopped at a second-hand tape stall and you told me about some of the bands I hadn't heard of. I asked you about Transponder.

"No," you said. "They're not heavy metal. They're more – have you ever listened to Pink Floyd?"

I hadn't, but resolved to.

"Like that. Not that they've been signed up yet. But they're effing brilliant."

You went on about them and it was great to see you being so enthusiastic. Like a kid. To look at, you were quite hard and threatening with your leathers and punk hair. You were twitchy, like they were out to get you. And it didn't sit right to me, because all the Asian boys I knew hung round together and were into hip-hop and rap and bhangra. You were by yourself but looked like them. We passed an Asian posse just outside the market and they eyed you oddly too. You walked straight past them. Maybe that was because you were with me, a white girl.

Part of me was wondering what was going to happen next between us. I felt really comfortable with you, and liked the person I was when I was with you. I was pleased you weren't all over me and just seeing me as a girl. I sort of fancied you then, but I didn't want to risk having a relationship as such – I knew relationships came with sell-by dates. I wanted more that that; I wanted to have you securely in my life. I was interested in you. I hadn't met anyone like you before. You were the only good thing to have happened to me for months.

When we got to the bus station there was an embarrassing silence.

"Where are you going now?" I asked you.

"Home. Then down the pub."

"Yeah. Me too. I mean home."

"We're going into town on Saturday night. We're meeting in The Pickled Rat at nine. Do you know it?"

"Yeah, I think so. By the Odeon."

"Can you come?"

"Yeah," I said.

"Great," you said. "See you there." And waved as you walked off to your bus stop.

It was enough. We were going to see each other again. It would be easy to lie to my parents. At last I had something to look forward to.

To Taz (3)

That Saturday night luck was on my side. My parents were going out for dinner and Mum was nagging Dad to get out of the bathroom. She wasn't paying any attention to me. That meant I could be vague about my plans. I told them I was seeing my friends, and going on to a party, so could I take some booze with me?

"Whose party?" Mum shouted down from the bedroom.

"A boy at school. A friend of Lucy's boyfriend, Brad."

"She should be buying her own booze," came Dad's voice from behind the bathroom door.

"With what?" questioned my mother, for once sticking up for me. "Since we won't let her get a Saturday job, she doesn't have money of her own."

"Thanks, Mum," I shouted back.

I went to the drinks cupboard and saw an unopened half bottle of vodka. Perfect. I put it in my bag together with some miniature bottles of Greek spirit that had been there for ages. Then I scrawled a note and left it on the kitchen table saying I didn't know what time I'd be in, but Lucy and I would share a taxi. I told Mum about the note, unlocked the front door and breathed in gallons of chilly, fresh air. Freedom.

Of course I was a bit nervous about meeting you in The Pickled Rat. There was a chance I wouldn't get in, and then what? But otherwise I felt good. Now we'd broken up my problems there were on hold, almost non-existent. I was living for the moment. I loved being on my own, accountable to no one.

The bus dropped me off quite near The Pickled Rat. As I entered, the sour, beery smell hit me. It was quiet, nothing playing on the juke box, just some old punks over in a corner and a few couples. No sign of you. I checked my watch and decided not to worry. I was five minutes early.

Time goes slowly when you're waiting. I stood near the door hoping no one would tell me to go. Every time someone came in a blast of cold air hit me. The barman looked at me curiously. I focused on the spirits behind the bar, the huge bottles of Teacher's whisky, Gordon's gin, Vladivar vodka and Bacardi suspended upside down. When Mac, Steve and the crowd came in I was relieved and looked for you among them, but you weren't there.

My stomach felt hollow. I wasn't sure what to do. At that stage I'd never spoken to Steve or Mac and was too shy to go up to them and ask where you were. I thought I'd hang on for you, maybe get myself a drink or something. I waited until they'd been served, and got myself a vodka and Slimline tonic. That was nearly half my money, but I didn't want to draw attention to myself by stopping the order.

I sat in a table by a corner where I could see the door. I was glad I was served without any fuss. I decided that if you didn't turn up soon, I would speak to your friends, but not immediately, not now.

Then some revolting old bloke in a suit with wispy, greasy hair came over, leering at me. He asked me if I was on my own, and I said I wasn't, but I think he could tell I was lying. He said he owned a club across the road and if I liked I could get in free. I said I wasn't interested. I got hot and bothered as he looked me up and down, his eyes resting on my boobs. I willed him to go away but I didn't want to cause a fuss. I glanced over desperately to Mac and Steve, but they were all laughing at some joke. So I drained my vodka and left the pub.

I looked down the road. Still no you. This was all going wrong. Only the last thing I was going to do was go home. So I wandered up to the late-night chemist and spent ten minutes or so in there, looking at the make-up and hair dye. Then I went back to The Pickled Rat, not feeling too cheerful. Steve and Mac had gone, so had the creepy bloke, but you still weren't there.

I left The Rat and stood outside on the street, watching people get off the bus opposite, in case you were on it. A girl stared at me. She was alone too. I thought she must be cold as her legs were bare and her coat ridiculously short. Then her gaze left me and she wandered along the road.

I wasn't scared, being alone like that. There were lots of people on their way to the Odeon and it was only quarter to ten. I was just upset that you'd stood me up. I thought you'd liked me and that we had already started being friends. Part of me was still sure you'd turn up. Another part of me liked just standing there watching everyone. It was a kind of escapism. Because when you look at other people and think about them, you forget yourself.

My hands were stuffed deep inside my coat pockets. I wiggled my toes so they wouldn't get too cold. I read the titles of the films being screened at the Odeon and tried to decide which one I'd choose if I had to see one of them. I tried to see if I could read the films backwards. But how do you pronounce 'eht'? 'Et'? Or 'e-h-t' – are there rules? An ambulance with its siren blaring and lights flashing parted the traffic and swerved round the corner. I watched it as far as I could.

Another bus poured out passengers who had reached their destination. I walked towards them, a gush of warm air billowing round my feet as I passed a basement kitchen. I resolved to go back and stand there, but it turned out not to be necessary. Because there you were.

You saw me immediately and apologised. I could tell straight away something was wrong, and knew that I wasn't the problem. Your face was tense and hard and your eyes wild. Your hair was messy and you'd slung on an old parka. Then you told me there was trouble at home.

"What trouble?" I asked.

"I just want to effing forget about it," you said. I could relate to that.

"Shall we go back to the pub?"

You consulted your watch.

"No – we'll go on to The Revolution."

I'd never been to The Revolution. Last year at school it was the in place to go. That is, if you liked heavy metal. Last year, though, I was busy working for my GCSEs, ten of them. As well as Grade 6 on the oboe. There wasn't much opportunity to go out, and anyway, I used to be a little scared of those sort of places. Like, people took drugs!

When we got there I realised I didn't have enough money to get in, as it was a fiver. You didn't seem to care and gave me the extra. Your face was still tight and you hadn't really looked at me. Whatever it was that had bothered you had really got a grip.

We went through the foyer into the room where the music was coming from. I thought I recognised Korn playing. I saw a pile of coats and bags in one corner and I was surprised that people just left them there. But no one was dancing. I always thought it would be really wild, really manic in The Revolution, but there were just a lot of moshers sitting around on the floor. There were chairs and benches along a wall, but some of them were broken and tatty, the kind of old, wooden chairs you'd expect to see in a church hall. There was a DJ on the stage but even he looked bored. The floor was filthy and old plastic bottles rolled at my feet. The people in the club seemed quite young. I wasn't sure what to do now. It was all a bit depressing. I guessed you were looking for your mates, but I couldn't see them. The music was too loud for us to talk. Eventually you went to sit on one of the chairs. I sat by you, undoing my coat.

I thought about offering you some of the vodka I had with me, but I guessed we wouldn't be allowed to drink it. I stole glances at you and saw your face was like thunder. I was at a complete loss. After a while I reached out and held your hand, just to reassure you someone else was there. I was glad that you gave my hand a small squeeze. I knew my gesture of support had been accepted.

I forget how long we sat there. Half an hour? Three quarters? Eventually you said, eff this, and I followed you out of the club. To be honest, I was glad to get out on to the street. The Revolution was a bit of a dump. You seemed to read my mind.

"It's crap there now," you said. "Full of kids and old rockers."

"Do you wanna go somewhere else?"

"No cash," you said. I felt guilty, then remembered my vodka. I opened my bag and showed you and your face held a glimmer of interest.

"I know where we can go," you said. You took my hand and hurried me along the street. We left clubland and passed the garish yellow lighting of McDonalds. We turned left and climbed up a narrow street to the old railway station. You knew how to get round the back and we clambered over planks and crushed Coke cans and squeezed sideways through a break in the wall. Then we climbed some more through some weeds and stuff until we reached the place where the line used to run. Luckily the wind had dropped a little so we weren't so cold. We sat down. Below us were all the roofs of the office buildings, the Odeon, street lights. I could imagine all the people beneath them, intent on their own business. We were alone and apart from it all. Down there all the people were doing their crazy stuff. Up here we were forgotten about. I took out the vodka, opened it, and passed it to you.

"You first," you said, smiling at me. It was the first time you'd smiled that night. I took a large gulp. It was vile and brilliant all at once. I passed the bottle to you and you did the same. The distant hum of traffic. A rustle as a slight breeze bothered the branches on the nearby trees. You passed the bottle back to me. I welcomed the punch and lift of the alcohol. You snuggled up against me and I had a moment of pure contentment, of belonging.

"Thanks, Cat," you said.

To Dave (2)

Bit by bit Taz explained what had happened. You see, his grandma had died.

Not that he knew his grandma at all. He'd seen photos but that was it. Because when his mum decided to marry his dad, the family cut his mum off. Like, they didn't want to have anything to do with her. It's hard to get your head round that. To them, she was throwing away everything: her religion, her culture. She was rejecting them in favour of this bloke who worked in a factory, who drank in a pub, ate pork. They mourned for her as if she was dead. That's what Taz told me.

But I can see why she would have wanted to do that. Just because you're born in a family it doesn't mean they're going to suit you, does it? Like, you can't choose your family. But anyway, Taz's mum was regretful, but she was really into his dad, so it was OK. So Taz had grown up knowing about this other family he never saw, the ones that were responsible for the colour of his skin and the fact his mum got this faraway look in her eyes sometimes, or made chapattis for a surprise. His dad is all right, Taz said, but just a bit quiet. The sort of person who watches telly, reads the paper, doesn't say much, just sits there. His mum tried to teach Taz stuff about his religion and when he was little he liked the stories. And at school the teachers just assumed he was Muslim and it was easier for him not to say anything. At secondary school, though, he did normal RE and he just reckoned all of it was rubbish. Well, you can understand that. I noticed you had a cross tattooed on your arm, Dave. Does that mean you're a Christian? Weird.

But I'm going off the point. So a couple of days ago one of his aunties rang up – the one who secretly kept up contact, auntie Shaheen. His grandma had had a stroke; she was in the hospital. Hamira – that's his mum – was devastated. Taz said it was like she'd only seen her mum yesterday, she was that upset. And she wanted to go and visit her in the hospital. Frank – that's Taz's dad – said not to bother, no one would want to see her. But Hamira wouldn't listen. Taz didn't want her to go to the hospital by herself so he went with her.

They made enquiries and found the right ward. Taz said they walked in past beds with screens round them not knowing which one the grandma was in, until Hamira clutched hold of Taz's hand. He saw all these women and one of them was his auntie Shaheen. The women of the family were all around the grandma's bed. And Hamira walked towards them, slowly, and auntie

Shaheen looked shocked and welcoming all at once, and they got to the foot of the bed, and the grandma sort of raised her head and had this startled look on her face. And before Taz had time to work out what it meant women were ushering his mum away from the bed, talking in their own language but it was clear enough what they were saying – go away, she doesn't want to see you, you're upsetting her, you're killing her – and Hamira began to cry in these gulping sobs. Taz said he wanted to smash someone's face in.

They sat in the corridor for a while and some nurses asked if they were all right, and Taz said yes, he was looking after his mum. And eventually they went home on the bus and she couldn't say a word. But when they got home she got her Koran out and sat there mumbling prayers. Frank told her to give over, that the past was the past.

Then that Saturday afternoon Shaheen rang to say the grandma had died. There was a big row in Taz's house because Hamira wanted to go to her father's house and help see to the body and Frank said she was daft, they wouldn't let her past the front door. But she was going on about it being her fault, her mother dying so young, she had brought grief on them, and Frank said she was mad. So did Taz. Then she said she would never be at peace if she couldn't be there. She broke away, went upstairs to find her salwaar kameez, and again it was Taz who went with her to her old family. His dad had given her up as a lost cause.

So they went round to the grandparents' house. The women washed and prepared the body there, then later the men went to the mosque for the funeral. When Taz's mum knocked on the door a couple of men answered it. Taz didn't know who they were. At first they didn't recognise her either, but then when they did it was terrible. They called her names, blocked the entrance, she was pleading with them, they looked at Taz like he'd just crawled out from under a stone. Taz swore at them, one of them got him by the collar and Taz was just about to lay into him when another older man came out – he guessed it was his grandad – and everything calmed down. He looked at Hamira and shook his head – there were tears in his eyes – and Hamira just turned and went. Taz went with her.

She tried to say the prayers at home but she couldn't for crying. Taz couldn't help because he didn't understand. Frank wouldn't turn the match off so they had to go into the bedroom. He got his mum to take some paracetamol and he tried to calm her down. He didn't want to leave her. Then later Frank came upstairs and apologised but said he knew this would happen. But he was being kinder then, and told Taz to beat it. So he got the bus into town hoping I hadn't got fed up waiting.

He told me all that when we were sitting on the

embankment, in between gulps of vodka. I got really upset for his mum. I told Taz my grandma had died too. It was three years ago, but it didn't affect us too much because she was living in a Home about sixty miles away. We only saw her once every six weeks when it was our turn. I was sad when she died and my mum was very brave. I didn't go to the funeral. Mum said it was well conducted and helpful. I can hardly remember my grandmother, only her elegant handwriting on my annual birthday card. So I said to Taz that I was like him, really, losing someone I never knew I had.

Then he was quiet for a long time. He's one of those people who keeps things bottled up and I knew even then it was amazing that he should have told me all that. I took it that he felt close to me and I was honoured. It means more, doesn't it, when someone opens up to you, than any success you might have, more than good grades, money, fame. So it muddled me, feeling good about being Taz's confidante, but bad on his behalf. Only I told him a kind of lie when I said I was like him, losing a grandma. Because as I was listening to him it was really his mother I was relating to. She did the same as me. Opted out. And it spooked me that she kind of regretted it. But I didn't want to go any further down that road. Instead I wanted to stay close to Taz, to cheer him up. It was hard to know what to do next. So I passed him the vodka again.

To Taz (4)

The vodka helped, didn't it? It changed your mood. And telling me helped too, I think. You were able to get it all out of your system. At least I hoped so. I felt sorry for you, I admired the way you stuck by your mum, and that made me like you more. I also looked up to you because I could see your life was hard in a way mine wasn't. You already knew stuff I didn't. And I reckoned it must be strange to look like one thing and be another. Because anyone looking at you would write you off as a typical Asian boy, but you weren't. That was like me too, I thought hazily. I look like a nice well brought up middle-class girl, but I wasn't. I mean, I didn't want to be, not any more. I wanted to choose.

OK, Taz, I'm lying. I don't suppose I had any of those thoughts then, that night. That's just how it seems to me now. What actually happened that night was that we got smashed. The more vodka we drank, the more foul it tasted. The Greek stuff was even worse and we had to drink it like medicine, holding our noses. We watched a helicopter with a searchlight looking up in the skies. You asked me to tell you about me.

I just said I was taking A-levels but I wasn't sure that was what I wanted to do now. You just listened. I said nothing made sense any more, and all the people around me made me angry, my parents, my teachers, even my mates. They led such narrow lives, they could only see in terms of their own rules. They couldn't see that people could be different to them, and that it didn't matter if they were. Maybe I was feeling your anger and I thought it was mine, just like I didn't know whether it was my hand inside your parka pocket or yours.

Then it was too much of an effort to talk so we did what any boy and girl would have done, we started to kiss. I remember the warmth of your mouth on mine and how nice it felt. We kissed, hugged, got as close to each other as we could. I wasn't at all scared of being alone with you like that. I really didn't care what happened.

Of course nothing happened. We were both pretty drunk. Once all the booze had gone there was a bit of an anti-climax. Then you said you were feeling better and it was still Saturday night and you were up for a good time now. I also felt a rush of energy. We stood up and hugged each other once more and kissed again, confidently, because we'd learned the shape of each other's mouths, we knew each other. Then we scrambled down the embankment laughing about something or other and feeling ridiculously happy. Soon we were back in town in a brilliant mood, finding everyone absurd and funny, the couple walking towards us in matching specs, the bloke on a bike with a headlight that kept flashing – you were going on about him flashing at us, which creased us up – anyway – we found ourselves in the centre of town without any money.

"I know where my mates are," you said.

So I followed you to Victoria Gardens. I knew people hung out there. Kids at school bragged about going to Victoria Gardens. It was just a scrubby open place in the centre of town that was too bare to be called a park, although there had been some attempt to grow grass there. Even the trees didn't look like proper trees but outgrowths of old wood, knotty, gnarled and tired. The moshers and other people sat on the benches. The bins were full to overflowing. Some old woman was rooting around in one of them. Then you saw your mates.

"Hey, look, it's the Paki," Steve said, but you smiled and didn't seem to mind.

We went over and you introduced me properly to Steve and Mac. I liked them immediately because they just accepted me. I was your friend and that was good enough for them. I was Cat. Nothing else mattered. They squeezed up to make room for us so you sat on the bench and I sat on your lap. They asked us if we had anything and I felt bad that we'd drunk all the booze between us. I would have liked to have had something to offer them. But there was a joint being handed round and eventually it came to you. You took a draw or two and handed it to me. Did you know that was the first time I'd even smoked a cigarette, let alone weed? I tried not to let it show. I copied what you had just done and held the smoke in my mouth. I tried not to cough. Then I passed it on.

No one said much. There was a bit of conversation about some people I didn't know, about some bloke who'd moved on to Sheffield. But otherwise we just all sat together. The together bit was what mattered. There were other people to watch, some drunks, a kid throwing up in the bushes, a group of girls who had come from a club and were gawping at us. Then I thought back to my other life at home and Victoria Gardens seemed unreal. Then I thought, hey, this is real, and my other life was the one that wasn't real. Like, who was Catherine Holmes anyway? The name was meaningless if you said it over and over again. What was I? Only a construct of my parents, a name on a list between Hill and Iqbal in the register at school. Cat was real, Cat who came out at night.

That little voice, that gnome, told me it was late, told me to look at my watch. It was almost too dark to read the time. 2.30am – as late as that. I knew I ought to think about getting home, only I didn't want to make the first move. And I couldn't imagine how I was going to get home. There were no late buses where I lived. You noticed I looked at my watch. You said you thought you ought to be getting home too.

So we walked. We walked out of town, along the New Road past the car showrooms, miles and miles, it seemed, hand in hand, and you watched me run down my road and let myself in with the key. And on the way home you memorised my phone number, and I memorised yours. As soon as I got to my bedroom, I wrote it down.

And my father came into my bedroom and said, we'll talk to you in the morning, young lady. Bang. The prison doors slammed shut.

To my mother (2)

Perhaps the next thing wouldn't have happened if you hadn't grounded me. Or perhaps it would.

My crime, apparently, was not ringing to let you know where I was. You had no objection, you said, to me staying out late, but you needed to know who I was with, where I was, and how I was coming home. At the time I thought you might as well plant a tracking device on me. What was the *point* of going out if I had to keep myself linked to home all the time? You were less bothered about the vodka I'd taken, and believed my lies about the party I went to being an all-nighter.

The idea was that if I was grounded, I would be so bored I'd catch up on my work. Fine, except now you'd given me a motive not to work – to spite you. OK, I know that's childish, but you and dad were pretty childish screaming at me because you didn't have the kind of daughter you wanted. *I don't know what's happened to you, Catherine! Do you understand the effect this is having on the family? I can't sleep, I'm so worried about you!*

OK. So it was Easter Monday. You'd invited round Auntie Megan and Uncle Joe as usual as well as some of Dad's Rotary friends. I had to be there too. The thought was like torture to me. Even in the olden days when I was a good little girl I got really bored at those sorts of gatherings. I was never sure what I was supposed to do at them. Just hang around, bring in trays of food and stand there while you boasted about me. When I was quite a bit younger I liked being boasted about, but in the last couple of years it had got dead embarrassing. Worst of all were Dad's friends who would look straight at my chest and say, Catherine's getting a big girl now. That's why I told you I was going to stay in my room.

I remember the look on your face when I told you that. Anger, but not just anger – there was fear too. I could see you were scared you couldn't handle me any more. I was pleased in a nasty sort of way, but I was scared too. Part of me wanted you to sort me out, to stay in control. The other part just wanted to defeat you. There was a stalemate. Then I had another idea, which, if I was clever, I could make out was a compromise.

"OK," I said, sounding as if I was climbing down. "But you've got to understand it's boring for me, with no one there of my age."

You saw what I was getting at and took the initiative.

"Do you want me to invite someone of your age?"

"Yeah."

"Who? Lucy?" Your tone of voice was conciliatory – pleased, even.

"Well, I was thinking of a new friend of mine. A boy, actually."

Mothers are so transparent. I could see your mind working. You hadn't bargained for a boy, but on the other hand if you could get this boy into your territory, so to speak, and find out what he was like, you'd know what you were dealing with. It would be far less embarrassing for you than having me locked up in my room while all the guests were there. I knew I was in a strong bargaining position.

"Do I know this boy?"

"No. He's a friend of Brad's. My age," I said. "Taking A-levels."

"What's his name?"

"Taz – it's a nickname."

"Taz!" You laughed indulgently. "Well, all right." You picked up the paper again but I could tell you weren't reading it. You put it down again a minute later. "So, this Taz," you continued. "Is he your boyfriend?"

I wish I knew. I honestly couldn't say.

"No," I replied. It was the safest answer. A few kisses meant nothing. And besides, the last thing I wanted was you probing, and giggling, and telling everyone that Catherine's got a boyfriend. Not that my reluctance to say anything stopped you telling Megan. I don't blame you – she is your sister. I guess if I'd had a sister, I would have told her everything. Did you know I overheard you?

You two were in the kitchen preparing the food. I had actually come down to help you, had put my hand on the doorknob and realised you were talking about me. So I stopped. Then I found I couldn't tear myself away.

"It's so out of character! My greatest worry is that there's something physically wrong with her. It had even crossed my mind that it's chronic fatigue syndrome as she seems so listless, but she goes out for long walks, and was out very late the other night. But on the other hand, she sleeps in for hours, and she still isn't working, Megan. Or maybe it's even a form of depression. If so, I can't think what has triggered it. Everything was going so well at school. After those superb GCSE results we were certain that Oxford or Cambridge was on the cards. She has everything going for her! She's always been so bright, so hard-working. Why should she suddenly switch off? I wondered if she was in with the wrong set of friends, but they're the same friends she's had throughout school, and they're all working. I even thought she might be experimenting with drugs. That's still at the back of my mind. I think I'll have to have a talk to her. Because I can't accept that she should throw away everything just on a whim. That makes no sense at all. There has to be a reason.

And you can imagine how this makes me feel. To watch my only daughter, with so much promise, risk so much. I thought we were so similar, so close. I thought she was just another version of me. What hurts most is that she won't explain, Megan! That she won't see sense. That she doesn't seem to understand what I'm going through. Yes, I will pour myself another glass of wine. It's not too early, is it? I need something to fortify me while I prepare the cake. It's as if she's deliberately set out to hurt me. And it's not as if she can catch up that easily. If she has to repeat her AS-levels next year, then that means an extra year's school fees, and where are we going to find those? Peter was hoping to retire. She doesn't think about that, does she? The young are so selfish. My only hope, Megan, is this boyfriend of hers. Maybe it was all just hormones! Perhaps we should have encouraged her to go out with boys earlier. He'll bring some balance to her life. He sounds like a nice boy, at college, she tells me. Her age. No, I haven't met him. Well, here's hoping he'll put her back on the straight and narrow. Hooray for men, that's what I say! Whoops! Is that slice of cake retrievable? Better put it in the bin. Do you think I should have a coffee before the guests arrive?

Yes, I heard all that. And I thought, if I'm so like you, I can get pissed too. So I went into the living room and poured myself a large sherry. Drank it, then poured another. I needed it. I felt awful about inflicting you and all of this on Taz, but I had to see him. Because I was grounded, it was the only way I could think of.

Dad and Uncle Joe came in from the garden then and found me drinking. They just said to pour something for them, which I did. Uncle Joe felt in his pocket and gave me a twenty-pound note.

"Buy yourself an Easter egg with this," he said.

I thanked him. I've always liked Uncle Joe. God knows what he saw in Auntie Megan. Or how she 'lowered herself' to marry him. Even though really he owns a factory where they make bathroom accessories – yes, toilet roll holders, loo brushes, and the like – Auntie Megan always says he's 'in business'. You can't even mention what Uncle Joe does for a living unless you turn it into a joke. Uncle Joe was always dead generous with me, though. We had a little chat.

"So how old are you now, Catherine?"

"Seventeen," I said, amicably.

"Seventeen. You should be learning to drive. We gave Brian and Nick driving lessons for their seventeenth birthdays. Both passed first time. Then Brian pranged Megan's car." He laughed at the memory. "So are you going to learn?"

"I might do," I said.

"Girls are less interested in motors than men," Uncle Joe said as an aside to my father. That riled me.

"Not so," I said. "Quite a few of my friends at school

are learning, and Melissa's actually passed her test. She did an intensive course."

And didn't we all know about it? Her parents had even bought her a second-hand Mini as a runabout. She had it fitted with a CD player.

"I must move with the times," Uncle Joe said, genially enough. "And it gives a girl a lot more freedom to have a car. Less dangerous than using public transport. Though when I was a lad..."

I'm sure you don't want me to repeat the rest. Uncle Joe's reminiscences could bore for Britain.

The guests started to arrive then. I was on red alert, waiting for Taz. I hoped he hadn't lost his nerve. I could hardly blame him if he had. You and Dad's friends were the pits. Sorry. I know they're probably nice people and everything and I accept I don't know any of them that well, but together they just depressed me. They were so stiff. And it was all small talk. The weather, holidays, the sales at John Lewis's – it was just talking for talking's sake. Like, I thought none of you really cared about each other. Well, I knew you didn't. I knew you and Dad had invited the Rotary chairman and his wife, Ted and Valerie Porter, even though you couldn't stand them. You felt *obliged*. There you were air-kissing Valerie and complimenting her on the suit she was wearing.

I offered to pour the drinks. I abandoned the sherry as it was pretty sickly, and moved on to the wine. Where was Taz? I was lost in a sea of flowery dresses and designer handbags, and men in suits with swollen paunches, tinny laughter, pathetic plates of finger food that the women were guzzling down while pretending not to be eating, a guffaw of laughter, clinking glasses, and you in the middle of it all, half-cut, looking both pleased and frazzled. At that moment my mood was precariously balanced. If Taz came, I would be on a roll, reckless; if Taz stood me up I would be finished, destroyed.

Only I heard the doorbell because of the volume of noise. I wriggled out of the crowd and opened the front door. Taz hadn't let me down after all. We just smiled at each other. Really smiled. I wanted to kiss him but didn't. I knew I was more drunk than he was and I wanted him to catch up with me. He'd made an effort with his appearance. He was wearing black combats and a black vest top and his leather jacket. He'd spiked up his hair with gel and I reached out and touched it.

"Cool!" I said. I took in his olive skin and dark brown eyes and thought that Taz was beautiful, in a way. Men can be beautiful too. I don't think beauty is just an attribute of women. I thanked him for coming because I realised that he must be feeling nervous. I was nervous on his behalf and I hoped I hadn't been selfish inviting him.

And then it started. I took him into the living room and went up to you, and said, "This is Taz!"

The look of shock in your eyes. The way the people in your group looked at you to see what your reaction would be. The way you tried to cover up your shock.

"Taz! How nice! Catherine has told me so much about you!"

Except, I thought, that he was Asian.

Taz was all tensed up, cracking his knuckles again. You just kept coming out with this crap about how lovely you were able to come, did you find the house easily? You were playing for time so you could recover your composure. Taz's eyes were darting everywhere, taking in all the plates of food, the piano, the country garden style three-piece suite and all the polite haw-hawing from your guests. I took his hand and squeezed it.

"Taz?" said Ted Porter, who had been busy chatting you up. "What's that short for?"

"Tariq," he mumbled. I knew he was squirming with embarrassment and I felt selfish for bringing him.

"Tariq. Ah. You wouldn't be Dr Patel's son? Good chap, ears, nose and throat."

"Patel is a Hindu name," I interrupted. "Tariq's family is Muslim." I couldn't be bothered to be entirely accurate.

"Pardon *me!*" Ted Porter said, humouring me. "So what branch of medicine does your father practise in, Tariq? Or is he a GP?"

"He's not a doctor," Taz said. "He had a job in a distribution warehouse but he's been laid off."

Ted Porter glanced at you in surprise, and you raised your eyebrows – my God! It was as if you had forgotten we were both there. Being drunk is no excuse, Mum. All my life I've been brought up not to be rude and there you were being such a snob – and showing it in public. In a way, it was funny. I realised that Taz's colour wasn't an issue. If his father had been a consultant surgeon or company director he could have been lime green, you'd have still been delighted to see him.

I was so staggered by your rudeness I didn't react. Not then, at any rate. Instead I led Taz over to the drinks table.

"Sorry about this," I muttered. "I know they're all awful. Why don't we go into the garden?"

Taz agreed, so I uncorked a bottle of red wine, took two glasses, and we went through the kitchen into the garden. It was better then.

"It's nice out here," Taz said. He wandered over to the pond and looked at the fish. I poured some wine and handed him some. I was aware that there were people standing at the French windows, and some of them were looking at us. I wanted to get away. I took Taz for a tour, showing him your herb garden and the rockery, and we wandered down to the shed. Taz turned and looked back at the house.

"You live in an effing mansion," he said.

"It sucks," I told him. He looked at me oddly then. I

realised to my amazement that he was quite impressed. That kind of upset me. I wanted him to hate you and the house as much as I did. Taz was mine, after all.

We sat down on the bench at the back of the garden and I poured the wine and we sat there drinking it. We just chatted to begin with. Taz explained about his father's problems at the warehouse, and how his mother was going to do extra hours at Asda as a result. I whinged about you and the fact there was all this pressure on me to work.

"Why aren't you working?" Taz asked me.

I was already pretty pissed by that stage and I think that's why his question made me angry. For a minute I thought even Taz was saying I ought to pull myself together. That I was just an over-privileged, spoilt kid. I wanted to try to explain to him that there was more than one way of feeling that you'd missed out. So I said there was more to life than essays. That I felt as if I was on an assembly line in a factory and before I knew it I'd be labelled in a box, just another commodity. That nothing I could do was going to be good enough. I could feel my anger now shifting to self-pity. I wanted to cry but I couldn't. I told Taz I wanted to have a life of my own. That I hadn't been given a chance to grow up.

Then I thought that Taz was my chance. I didn't say that to him. Instead I carefully put my wineglass on the grass, turned to him, and kissed him. I didn't give a damn who saw. He kissed me back, but it wasn't like it was up on the embankment. He felt tense, he was holding back. I blamed you, Mum – that's not as crazy as it sounds. Taz wasn't himself because everyone had been so mean to him. Especially you. Whereas before I had been letting go, letting the wine dissolve my anger, now it came back in a rush. I wanted to be alone with Taz and I couldn't. And I'd brought Taz from my world into yours, and you'd shown me you despised him. Crazy thinking, maybe. But I hadn't eaten much all day except for some chocolate in the morning and the wine was giving me a headache. Perhaps I shouldn't have mixed the red wine with the sherry and white wine I'd had earlier.

So Taz and I got up and walked some more around the garden. Then we saw you and Dad coming towards us with the Porters. It was all becoming a nightmare. Dad was wittering on about security and Neighbourhood Watch and the break-ins there'd been recently. Ted Porter nodded furiously. I mean, what subject could be more important than the good old middle classes keeping hold of their own.

Drink does funny things to you. I was beginning to see that. It makes you happy, it can make you very tired, it also kids you that you sound brilliant when you don't. You think you're being clever when in fact you're coming over like an idiot. But it also stops you caring what other people think. It lets you say what's on your mind. So blame the drink, not me.

"Taz and I are going out for a while," I told you. I didn't want to stay in your party for one moment longer.

"No, honey," you said, looking daggers at me. "Remember you said you were going to stay in and help me tidy?" You meant, you're grounded, Catherine.

"Let her go," Ted Porter said, waggishly. "I daresay she has things to say to her young man."

What a creep! He made my skin crawl.

Then Dad intervened. "Sorry, Ted. You're a sport to stick up for her, but I'm afraid Catherine's under house arrest. There's a small matter of some essays and a couple of pieces of coursework."

Ted winked at me. "There are more important things than school. I'm going to stick up for Catherine here, Peter. I never got myself any qualifications, and that didn't hold me back. It's character – character and determination. Those are what count, in the final analysis. I didn't get where I am today by sitting exams. Oh, no. Seize the day, Catherine. Carpe diem. And Tariq, what about you? What are your plans in life?"

I squirmed for Taz. He shrugged, embarrassed.

"I'm interested in art," he said.

"Art! Now there's a subject! I don't go in for all this modern stuff, you know. Give me a good old portrait or landscape. Constable. Turner. The Mona Lisa. There's nothing wrong in being old-fashioned, Tariq. Get yourself grounded in the basics. Start from the bottom. Like I did. Don't be afraid of getting your hands dirty."

Ted Porter was itching to talk about himself, I could tell. It amused me to prompt him.

"You began as an errand boy, didn't you?" I said.

Ted Porter preened himself. "Errand boy. Then office junior. Then clerical work. Once they saw what a smart lad I was, it was onwards and upwards. Deputy manager, manager, director, on the board, a partner – Huitt and Porter Properties. I can't pretend I've not been successful. But I'm grateful for it, oh yes! I've always done my bit for charity. Can't forget those less fortunate than oneself. This will interest you, Tariq. I was in India a couple of years ago, a bit of a holiday. Now, *there* was poverty. Cripples on the street, children begging. I'm surprised their parents let them. But then, foreigners aren't like us. I don't mean you, Tariq. I can see you're assimilated. And some of my best friends are of Asian origin. I respect them. They know a thing or two about hard work. Make sure you work hard, Tariq."

Something snapped then. I'd had enough.

"Don't you be so... so bloody patronising! You're so up yourself! Just because you're old, it doesn't give you the right to talk down to us! I know you stand around at meetings wearing chains and medals and toasting the Queen and shaking hands with other fat old slobs, but you're still not anything special. In fact you're more childish than we are. It's all games with you. You know nothing about real life. You're so satisfied with your silly little world where everyone has to look up to you that you write off whole cultures. And I'm supposed to model myself on people like you? You're ignorant, you're racist... you're disgusting!"

And by that I meant all of you.

"Catherine!" I remember the horror in your voice. But I didn't feel as if I'd done anything wrong. The opposite, in fact; I felt as if I was a sword blade glinting in the sunlight, slashing through swathes of hypocrisy, fighting for the truth.

"And it's not just you. It's everybody..." I made a sweeping gesture to the lounge where people were still eating and drinking. "They're like rats in a cage. Only they don't realise it. And they preach to us and never think to look at their own prejudices and faults. I think..." I was struggling now. I wanted to make an impact and couldn't work out how. The booze was making me fuzzy. "I think – you're all jealous. You want to be young again. Well, you're not. I am, and I'm not wasting my time like you." Waves of fury and nausea were coming over me. I could see the shocked look on everyone's faces. Then Dad's hard, murderous eyes and Ted Porter's astonished, gaping mouth gradually lost clarity.

"Catherine. Apologise," you said.

Next, a heaving in my chest and I didn't have time to get back into the house. I could only get as far as the azalea bush, and I threw up there.

To Lucy

"And I threw up behind the azalea bush! Everyone totally freaked. Well, not Taz. He was dead sweet and put his arm round my waist, and handed me his handkerchief afterwards. The thing that I was most worried about was that it would put him off me. And we didn't have time to talk because my parents packed me up to my room and told Taz to beat it. Well, not to 'beat it', exactly. They were polite to him, but it was clear what they were thinking."

You looked amazed. I found I was enjoying telling you the story. Also it made it seem more like an escapade, a mad thing I had done. I felt it gave me some kind of credibility. I deliberately didn't tell you not to broadcast it; I wanted it to get around. We were sitting on the grass outside the tennis courts. It was break. You'll remember. Our conversation was important to you, too.

"So then what did your parents do?" you asked.

"Don't remind me! It was like, the biggest lecture I'd ever had in my life. They stood over me while I wrote the Porters an apology, and then started with, exactly *how* much did you have to drink? So it was pretty awful all holiday. And they tried to blame it all on Taz. Said I was obviously mixing with the wrong sort of people."

"Did they stop you from seeing Taz?" you asked, alarmed.

"I've been ringing him. And now we're back at school it'll be easier. I'm no longer grounded."

"Poor you," you said. You meant it. You couldn't imagine anything worse than being separated from a boyfriend.

That was why I'd chosen you to talk to. I think we all do that – have different friends for different aspects of our life. There are things I wouldn't tell you about, and there are probably things you wouldn't tell me about. But if it was anything to do with boys or fashion or the gossip on the latest boy band, or what's hot in cheesy music, you're my first port of call. Don't get me wrong. I'm not being disrespectful. You're one of the people I like most because you're so affectionate and undemanding.

When I'm with you, I find myself growing like you. You're infectious, in the best sort of way. I become all girlie too. The difference between us is that you really are sweet and innocent. I only pretend to be. With me it's a mask. One of my masks. Because even now I can't say who I truly am, or more accurately, who I intend to be. But hey, let's not get heavy!

So I changed the subject and asked you about Brad, and as we talked I pulled daisies from the grass and made a chain, like we did when we were small. You were earnest, relieved and glad to answer my questions.

"How long have you been going out now?"

"Six weeks," you said. "Six weeks and three days to be precise. I can't believe it, really."

"What can't you believe?"

"Oh, I don't know. That someone like that would want to go out with me. He is like, so sweet. He sends the cutest text messages. Look." You got out your phone and showed me your message archive. You'd been storing his messages. I was glad to see he was as soppy about you as you were about him. It made me smile and cheered me up.

"What's that one about?" I asked. "*Don't worry. I can wait.*"

"Guess," you said archly.

"Does he want you to sleep with him?"

"Oh, you guessed! Yeah, he does. It's quite flattering, I think."

I laughed. "Very flattering. Now, for thirty-two thousand pounds, and remember – all your lifelines are gone – do *you* want to sleep with *him*?"

"Well, I think I want to."

"Is that your final answer?" I enjoyed kidding you.

"Stop it, Cath! Yeah, I will one day. Maybe soon, I don't know." You began to fiddle with the grass, pulling at individual blades. "But the thing is, I'm not sure what to do."

"Use a condom," I said, knotting two daisy stalks.

"I know *that*! But it's more like, what if I'm no good at it?"

"It's not an exam," I said to you, laughing. You laughed too and tore up clumps of grass and flung them at me. I ducked. What with having you to myself, and the sunshine, and the juniors in the tennis courts thwacking balls around, I was starting to feel happy again. It was easy to pretend the exams weren't around the corner. Which they weren't. There was still six – or five – weeks to go.

The teachers had been laying off me. It was almost as if they had this policy not to stress me out. I went to lessons – well, I skipped Economics – and sometimes joined in. I was wondering whether just going to the lessons meant I could pass the exams. I hadn't decided what to do about the exams. They loomed ahead like black rocks. But then, sitting on the grass with you, I forgot about them. Besides, something else was on my mind.

"No, seriously, Cath," you said. "I'd feel better if – if, like – I'd had some experience."

"Has *he* had experience?" I asked you.

"Well, no. He's a virgin too."

"So no problem."

You laughed in a strange way. I got the impression you didn't really want to sleep with him at all, but thought perhaps you ought to. I would have told you not to do it, I reckon, if it wasn't that it would make me the world's biggest hypocrite. Because I knew I wanted to sleep with Taz.

This is the bit you didn't know about, and the bit you'll find most interesting. So I'll tell you. I had this idea that sleeping with Taz would change me, that some way I would end up different. I didn't even mind if I was disappointed; I just had to find out. I didn't see what the big deal was, anyway. OK, it was important not to get pregnant or AIDS, sure, but after that, it's my body, mine to do with as I please. And I fancied Taz. I loved the colour of his skin. I loved the smell of his skin, like almonds. When we were close, I just felt as if I wanted to get closer. I thought sleeping with him would bring out something good in me, something loving. Most of the time I'd been going around hating everyone and everything, and I wanted to feel connected again. Unlike you, I wasn't nervous about sex. I mean, it's natural, isn't it? It was more a matter of getting the opportunity. I knew how to get condoms – the young people's drop-in in town doled out freebies. But how could Taz and I get to be alone?

The other problem was that he hadn't asked me to sleep with him. Or rather, I couldn't honestly say that we were going out, that we were an item. He'd not asked me to be his girlfriend. It was all kind of assumed. We didn't need to label what was happening. I was certain he cared for me, and equally certain he was as curious about sex as I was. But we hadn't spoken about it.

For you and Brad it was different. A lot of what you did, you did in the public eye. You boasted about him to us, the girls at school, and we quite liked it because everyone likes a happy romance. I'd got wind of the fact he boasted about you too, but in a slightly different way. I reckoned as soon as you slept with him it would be all round the common room. Well, it was. And you didn't mind, you were proud in your way. You told me first, and I appreciated that. You told me in the toilets before school. You said it was nothing really, and over very quickly. But yes, you did feel different. More grown-up, you said. And closer to him. And you asked me if I'd slept with Taz.

I was dreading that question. Then Fliss and Toni came in and broke up our chat. I was incredibly relieved. You just took it for granted we *had* slept together, and never asked when or how it happened.

Now's the time to tell you. I know you'll understand.

To Lucy (2)

I began to see quite a lot of Taz. My parents weren't a problem because I'd discovered how good I was at lying. The skill is in *believing* that what you're saying is true, whatever it is. And who's to say it's not going to happen anyway? I mean, I could tell you a green elephant is coming towards you, and you couldn't totally rule out the possibility that one might.

I can just see your face now, Lucy. Your forehead wrinkled and eyebrows raised, looking at me as if I'd really lost the plot.

Perhaps I have.

I told my parents I was going out with a crowd of friends, and I knew they were uneasy. But they also recognised that since I was seventeen and doing nothing illegal, they could hardly stop me. Taz was hard up most of the time and so we thought about going into clubs, but mostly we didn't. Mostly we hung around town. His mates sit in the park, or Victoria Gardens. It's true they're out of it most of the time. That is, when they can get hold of anything,

White Lightning, Special Brew, nail varnish, weed, whatever.

When they do, they pass it round. Sharing like that makes you feel close to everyone, part of them. They're good people, Lucy, and it makes me angry how society labels them as failures and outcasts just because they don't conform. Like, Bex was in care but now she lives with her aunt. She was crap at school because she was dyslexic but now she does some waitressing. Only she has to take out all her piercings before she goes into the café in case it puts the punters off. Mac is kind of in between jobs because he wants to get his head together. Really he wants to help people, like the disabled or something, but he doesn't know how to get into that. He gets dosh by hair braiding in the market sometimes. Steve is at college with Taz and doing computing but he doesn't like it. We all talk, about anything. And this is what's different about them – they don't diss each other. You know how at school everyone's bitching about everyone else, and the boys are as bad as the girls? How nothing you do is private? How there's all that boasting and girls eyeing you to check out your clothes? There was none of that with Taz's crowd. Maybe I didn't know them that well, but I doubt it. One night a mate of Bex joined us and he was really losing it, screaming, having hallucinations. They were brilliant, talking to him, and then taking him to the hospital and staying with him all night. That's the kind of people they were. When I was with them, I felt safe. I know you think I'm weird, and that you would never do drugs and that, but you drink, don't you? And have coffee? And we know Melissa smokes. So everyone's just as bad as each other, and the people who pass judgements are the worst of all. That's what I think, anyway.

Taz and I were seen as an item. If I turned up without him, people asked me where he was. When we were alone we talked and talked, about his family, mine, about music, about other people. Never properly about us, and I didn't want to. At school I was fed up with all this *who's going out with who* business. Like, why should it matter if you have a boyfriend or not? And why is it everybody else's business? So Taz and I drifted together. He was like a male version of me. My best friend. My more than best friend because he was so different. And with all the hassle I was getting from school, I really valued having him.

And, yes, I did want to sleep with him. I imagined, like the rest of our relationship, it would just happen naturally. The trouble was, we were rarely alone. If we were, it was on the streets. I couldn't take him to my house and he'd never suggested going back to his. For a start, his father was there most of the time. It seemed a liberty to go back to Mac's place just to have sex. Kind of dirty in the wrong way. So nothing happened for a couple of weeks.

And all the time my parents and school were making out that I had to listen to them, they knew best, they were older than me, wiser, adult.

I can do adult, I thought.

Then the opportunity I was waiting for happened, quite naturally. Taz said that his parents were both going out on Sunday. His dad's brother was having a fiftieth celebration, and he was glad, because it would cheer up his parents. He was staying in, he said, to finish off some art. He was doing some still lifes – but not the usual sort. It was a project on rotting fruit – studies over a period of weeks. I'd been watching them develop and it's strange how you can find beauty in very ugly things when you suspend your judgement. Mould is all shades of green and grey and textured like curly fur. And so the stage was set for the big seduction scene.

I prepared myself carefully. Yeah, all the usual stuff: long, hot bath, perfume, hair just right. I'd got some condoms from the drop-in and I'd also bought a bottle of vodka. It's easy. I look eighteen and the trick is to go into the offie as if you have every right to be there. And don't say, *can I have some vodka?* But ask for it by brand. *A bottle of Vladivar, please.*

I took the bus to the estate where Taz lived, early in the evening. It wasn't dark then. I'd passed by the Meredith estate lots of times, but never walked through it before. People say it has a bad reputation, but there's no evidence of it. There's graffiti, sure, and kids hanging around on bikes giving you evils. The houses are quite modern, not the old red-brick terraces but little maisonettes, some with net curtains in the windows, and first-floor flats with washing hanging outside. Taz lived in Carlyle Point, a tower block. I knew exactly where it was as I always made a special point of looking for it when I passed on the bus.

He lived on the eighth floor. I could have taken the lift but it smelt of piss and disinfectant. So I ran up the stairs, feeling unfit, my heart pounding, my leg muscles aching, my knees weak. There was no one about and dusk was descending. When I got to the eighth floor I stopped to catch my breath by leaning over the balcony and looking over town. The park opposite looked like an oasis of green even though I knew in reality it was scabby and litter-strewn. You could see all the way into town: the office blocks, the hotels. A cool wind fanned my face. The traffic was a long way down but the noise made it sound close. I bent right over and felt a weird exhilaration as I measured the drop. I had this urge to throw myself over, so then I straightened up.

I tidied my hair and made my way along the balcony until I found Taz's front door. Blue, tarnished letter-box halfway up, an electric buzzer. I buzzed, trembling. What would Taz's reaction be, seeing me unexpectedly?

Footsteps. Door opens. Taz. Lovely, beautiful Taz, in a

tight grey vest top, baggy trousers, hair groomed. He was startled to see me.

"Cat? Is something wrong?"

"No," I said. "I just felt like seeing you."

He laughed with a mixture of pleasure and surprise. He invited me in. The flat was kind of open plan, just a living room with a small kitchen on the right, from which came a spicy smell. The flat wasn't what I had expected at all. The carpet was a kind of electric blue colour. There was heavily patterned wallpaper. My parents would have thought it was tasteless but I wasn't sure. What was wrong with being loud? The TV and video looked quite new, although the paisley settee and matching armchair didn't. I noticed a table against the far window with plates and stuff on it that hadn't been cleared up. There were some cheap looking ornaments, no books. Taz had his eyes on me, knowing I was surveying his flat.

"Not quite like your place," he commented.

"I know, and I prefer it here. It's not so pretentious." Then I was scared I sounded patronising and found myself blushing. "Anyway," I continued, "it's you I wanted to see." I sat down on the settee. I could feel the springs cutting into me. Taz still stood and seemed on edge.

"Anything happen?" he asked.

"No." I unzipped my bag and brought out the vodka. "Look what I've brought."

"Where did you get that from?"

"I bought it. With some money I was given. And I've been getting a lift with Melissa to and from school, and saving lunch money."

"You've got to eat," he said, sounding just like my mother, but it was OK coming from Taz.

"Do you have any glasses?"

He went to the kitchen to get some while I noticed a corridor leading to what I guessed must be the bedrooms and a bathroom. I wished he would hurry up with the drink. I was nervous and getting more nervous by the minute. Maybe I should have planned this whole evening more carefully. I thought of you, Lucy, and reckoned had I taken you into my confidence you would have given me hints. You would have said that sometimes women have to take control. You were always talking like that, saying men do one thing, and women another, as if we were different species. I didn't entirely go along with that. Like, look at me and Taz. He was the bloke and about to be seduced. I was the seducer and didn't have a clue what to do.

He came back with two beer glasses. He said they were all he could find as his mum didn't drink and his dad just had beer or lager. I poured Taz a large drink as well as one for me. I took a large gulp. Immediately I felt better.

"So," I said.

He laughed again, his soft, teasing laugh. I reckoned he could read my mind. There was this atmosphere in the flat now, sort of erotic. A boy and a girl alone together. I knew I needed to push things on.

"Where are your pictures?" I asked. "I thought you were working on them."

"They're in my room," he said quickly.

"Your bedroom?"

He nodded.

"Can I go and see?"

"Yeah, OK."

We both got up and went to his room. The drawings were stacked against the wall. His bed was unmade, the duvet in a heap. A lovely smell of Taz in the room. Some of his clothes hanging over a chair. Books and papers on a table. I sat on the end of the bed.

"Haven't you started work yet?"

"No. I wasn't in the mood."

We both drank some more.

"Taz," I said. "I was missing you."

"No need," he said. He smiled at me and I should have felt better, but I didn't. I was a bit let down. It was something to do with Taz. He wasn't entirely being himself. It was like he was shut up. He was nice to me, pleased to see me, yeah, but closed. Not at home. Or maybe I was imagining it. Maybe it was just my nerves.

"Come here," I said. I drained my vodka – I wished I'd given myself a larger amount – and when he sat by me on the bed I put my arms around him and kissed him. There was that melting feeling in my stomach that spread to my legs. I began to rub his back. He kissed me back but didn't extend what we were doing. Christ, I thought, do I have to do all the work?

"You're wearing aftershave," I murmured, in between kisses.

He laughed again, a remote, preoccupied laugh.

More kisses. Less response.

"Taz. Are you all right?"

"Yeah. No. Like it's weird, you coming here like this. Having you in my room and everything."

I reached out and stroked his thigh over his trousers. His muscles were rigid.

"Sorry," I said. "I was wrong. I should have rung and let you know I was coming."

"It's OK," he said.

I looked to see if he needed more vodka as I certainly did. But Taz's glass was still half full. I went to fetch the bottle to the bedroom. Ought I to actually state what was on my mind? Taz and I were so close it ought to have been easy to talk to him about anything. But how could I say, I want to sleep with you?

I noticed on the bedpost a glass ornament that looked like an eye. I fingered it.

"It's to ward away the evil spirits," Taz said. "The eye of the Prophet. A present from my mother."

Then I noticed a dog-eared photograph pinned to a board, of a very pretty, large-eyed Asian woman with long, flowing hair, and a ruddy, chubby blond man next to her, towering over her.

"Your parents?" I asked.

Taz acknowledged they were. I realised then that the worst thing I could have done was draw attention to that photo. It was like I'd brought his parents right into the bedroom. I had some more vodka and was getting very light-headed.

"I'm sorry for barging in like this," I said, desperately. "But there is something. I mean – oh, hell, I don't know how to say this. Perhaps I should just come straight out with it."

"Yeah. Do." Taz looked worried, and I felt guilty for making him worried.

"Like, this is embarrassing, right?" I could hear myself sounding like the ditsy sort of female I detested most of all. I tried to sound more sensible, more thoughtful but the alcohol, as usual, was doing funny things to me. My voice, when it came, sounded as if it didn't belong to me, as if it was someone else doing the talking.

"I've been thinking that I'd like to... I wondered what it would be like... Taz – can we sleep together?"

He looked astonished. OK, I'd sprung it on him but I

thought he would get used to the idea very quickly. I mean, he's a bloke, right?

"Cat!" He put his hand on my shoulder. "Hey…"

"Because it's the right time, Taz. We're so close in every other way. I've brought some condoms but they're in my bag in the front room. I have thought about this. I won't regret it. I'm not doing it to trap you or anything. Kiss me!"

He did, long and lovingly, and I thought it was about to happen. And then the doorbell went. His parents, back early. What should I do? But it was OK – they wouldn't suspect anything – we were still dressed, and it would be easy to pass my visit off as long as I remembered to hide all traces of the vodka.

Only why would his parents use the buzzer?

Taz leapt up and raced to the door. It wasn't his parents but a friend. A bloke. I was curious, and taking the bottle with me I made my way into the living room.

The man was in his twenties or thirties, I couldn't tell which. He was dressed expensively in designer gear. Although his hair was slightly thin in the front, it was immaculate. A jacket was slung over his shoulders. I couldn't work out who he could be in Taz's life. His art teacher, maybe? Certainly not a relation.

"Cat – Spence," Taz said. God knows what this guy thought of me, clutching the vodka.

"I thought," said Spence, "that we were going out

somewhere?" He spoke to Taz, not me. Taz evidently knew him well. In that case, why hadn't he mentioned him to me? You see, Lucy, that was what hurt most.

"Yeah, we are," said Taz. "Cat just called round."

"Can we give you a lift somewhere?" Spence asked pleasantly.

I felt myself being nudged away from them.

"Uh... OK," I said. I didn't know where, though.

So Taz prepared to lock up and wouldn't meet my eyes. Spence chatted amiably about the weather, how it was improving, how quiet town was on a Sunday night. I slowly put my vodka in my bag. Taz took his jacket from a cupboard in the hall, a leather jacket that smelt new. I'd not seen it before. Here was someone acting like Taz, not my Taz at all. I walked with them down the stairs. Apparently they didn't use the lift either.

At the bottom was one of those little Smart cars in silver and orange.

"I can fit you both in if you move up, Taz," Spence said.

So we were jammed in together. Taz was unusually quiet, which had a knock-on effect on me. I was quiet too. Not surprising, as I had a lot to get my head round. I had been so sure Taz and I would sleep together tonight. But we hadn't. And I couldn't work out if I felt rejected or not. I certainly felt frustrated. Not sexually, but because the one positive thing I wanted to do had come to nothing. I was still a virgin, still a kid. Perhaps I'd been using Taz – but no, because I really liked him.

And in between working all that out, I was wondering who this Spence was and why Taz had never mentioned him before. I thought it would be a bit pathetic of me, a bit uncool, to ask directly who he was, or where they were going. I thought it would be more polite, anyway, to wait for an explanation. I was sure I'd get one eventually.

Spence asked me where I wanted dropping off.

"Anywhere in town," I said. I saw Taz glance at me, concerned.

Spence put some music on and then no one talked. It was wicked, driving into town like that, like we were in a movie. Spence was sophisticated and older and seemed OK – there was a smile playing on his lips, or maybe he was one of those people whose face, resting, sets in a smile. He parked the car round the back of John Lewis's. We all got out. The alcohol I'd had earlier was making me feel carefree, reckless. I didn't want to go home. I wanted to hang out with Taz and Spence. Spence picked up on that.

"You coming for a drink with us, Cat?"

"Cool," I said. I glanced at Taz. He glanced at Spence. There was a kind of mystery here which made it all the more interesting. Spence took the lead and we ended up at Satin, a bar I'd passed once or twice, didn't know much about. We walked down some steps, past posters of Hollywood stars. I recognised Marilyn Monroe and the film *Gone With The Wind*. There was another poster of a bloke with eye make-up and dressed like an Arab. Some film star from the past.

The bar was quite busy for a Sunday night. I sat at a table and asked Spence for a vodka and Slimline tonic. Taz went with him to the bar, and I looked around.

There were mostly blokes in the bar. They weren't the lager lout types; they were quite well-dressed, self-possessed. A few of them had shaven heads. I noticed a couple of blokes over in the corner and for a moment I could swear they were holding hands. I looked again. They were. I would point that out to Taz when he came back. Cool. I reckoned Spence had taken us to a gay bar, and I was glad. I'd never been in one before. There were a couple of women there, but they were with some blokes, so I didn't reckon the women were gay. They didn't look it, anyway.

Taz and Spence came back with drinks. I nudged Taz, pointed out the blokes at the other table who were still holding hands, and were now having a very intense conversation, looking into each other's eyes.

"Yeah," he said, brushing it aside. That irritated me. I could tell he was trying to be sophisticated in front of Spence. If Spence wasn't there, we'd have had a laugh about it. Not a cruel laugh, because I've got nothing against gays. In fact I like them – I mean – I think I would if I knew any. But it was the surprise, really. Walking into a bar and seeing two men as intimate as that.

"It's nice here," I said to Taz and Spence.

Spence got up, headed in the direction of the Gents. That gave me a chance to ask Taz some questions.

"Who is he?" was the first.

"A friend," Taz said.

"Where did you meet him?"

"In town."

"Why are you being so vague about it? And isn't he a bit old to be a friend?"

"I should have told you before," he said.

"Told me what? What haven't you told me?"

"About this other part of my life," he said, cracking his knuckles.

"Like you have older friends? It's a bit weird, but why is that a problem? Spence seems OK. I like him."

"Cat," Taz said. "He's more than just a friend."

More? I was puzzled. OK, Lucy, I know I was being dense, but I'd been drinking and with Taz and I having the sort of relationship we had, why would it cross my mind that he was gay? And maybe there was a kind of denial going on there too.

"More than just a friend? What do you mean? It sounds like he's your lover or something!"

It was Taz's silence that filled me in. I swallowed hard.

"Not my lover," he said. "Not yet. I haven't known him that long. Look, Cat, I'm not even sure where I want this to go."

I interrupted him. "But I thought *we* were going out together. Are you saying you like men too?"

He nodded.

"So you're what, bi—, bisexual?"

I felt I had to spell it out, so there could be no possible doubt.

"Maybe," he said.

"You mean you don't know? How can you not know what you are? I don't get it."

I saw that I was upsetting him. Part of me felt glad; he'd betrayed me and by hurting him I was making him feel my hurt. But I hated myself for being so cruel.

"Does this mean we're not going out together any more?" A childish, silly question I regretted the moment it left my lips.

"We can still be friends. Look, I don't know. Cat, please!"

"I'm sorry," I said. "I won't push you again. It's just that – I never expected this. All the things we've done – were you just pretending?"

"No, not at all."

I didn't know whether to believe him. Then Spence came back.

"Have you explained?" he said to Taz.

"He has," I said. "Thanks for the drink." I got up, a little unsteadily. "Don't worry about me," I said. "I'll get a taxi."

To Taz (S)

The worst thing was thinking that you didn't trust me enough to tell me you thought you might be gay. I'd imagined we were so close you could have told me anything and not been afraid of my reaction. If you'd broken it to me gently, it wouldn't have been such a shock. I would have been taken aback, I guess, but I would have got used to it. Honest. But finding out in the way I did left me spinning. One minute you were straight and fancied me, the next you were gay and fancied Spence. Well, OK, not gay but bisexual. Yes, I was upset, and it took some getting used to. I was hurt by the fact that you hadn't told me sooner. Did you think I was so straight and boring and narrow-minded I could never have accepted that you were confused about your sexuality? You made me feel our relationship had been a sham, that you didn't trust me. That you didn't like me as much as I liked you.

So I felt a fool, a proper idiot. Firstly, for not sensing the fact you were different. Then for just about everything that had happened that night. For my bizarre idea that you would want to sleep with me. For the fact I was crazy enough to set you up. For not realising as soon as Spence walked in the flat that *he* was gay – that should have been startlingly obvious. But I guess I'm just not used to stuff like that. And for going to Satin with you and never picking up for one moment that I was out of place, unwanted. I felt stupid, and betrayed. Angry with myself, and angry with you. And lonely. Because without realising it, you had become my best, my only true friend.

But lonely isn't a big enough word. It was more than that. I felt cut adrift. I'd left my old life and thrown in my lot with yours. Because you were so different I felt that just by being with you, *I* was different. That I was saying something about me because I chose to be to your almost-girlfriend. But now I was back where I started. A failed rebel. A rebel without courage. A rebel without you.

Sorry if this sounds over-dramatic, but it was what went through my head initially. Later, some time later, I saw my initial reactions had been selfish. *I* was angry, *I* was betrayed, *I* wasn't taken into your confidence. So I tried to think about you, and why you never had the courage to tell me you were bisexual. I guess it was easier for you to compartmentalise your life. It's easier to be one person at a time. When you were with me, you were one Taz, with Spence, another. With your parents, I reckon, another. A good way to live, because as soon as you get fed up with one side of yourself, you can morph into another. Multiple personalities. Several lives in one. It's naïve to think that anyone is just one person, that there's a *real* you. What is real? You can only exist in one moment, and then that moment is gone. And there's a new moment, a new you. And you can't even say you're the sum of all your parts, because you can never be all of your parts, all at once.

I guess I was glad to have at least one side of you. Maybe that was all you could ever have of anyone. Maybe relationships start going wrong when you want all of someone.

So I could see it from your point of view. I'd succeeded in rationalising the situation.

But the funny thing was, I still felt angry, stupid and betrayed. That was why I didn't get a taxi that night but went to Victoria Gardens to see if Mac and Steve and Bex were there. So in a way, it was because you let me down that I met Jan. A direct line connects you.

Look at me. I'm Cat, sometimes Cath, sometimes Cathy. And I'm Catherine too. No one can have all of me.

To Jan

That was the night I first met you – the night I walked out of Satin, rejected.

I made my way to Victoria Gardens, noticing that the streets were quiet, much quieter than Saturday. The people in town had a shifty air, as if they should have been at home in front of the TV or something. I knew there was a good chance Mac and everyone might not be in the Gardens but I didn't want to think as far as that. I just wanted to walk, to move away from what had just happened.

Got to the Gardens. There they were. Just Mac and Steve. I quickened my pace, my mouth preparing itself to smile. Steve acknowledged me with a nod. I sat by them.

"Where's Taz?"

"Somewhere or other," I said. Even though he betrayed me, I wasn't going to split on him.

"You two had a row?"

I shook my head. Steve and Mac seemed a bit down, not their usual selves. I didn't feel I knew them well enough to ask why. Steve was singing something slow to himself, tapping his foot on the asphalt. Mac just stared.

I looked around the gardens. Saw a man asleep on a bench, an overcoat over him. You were on the bench almost but not quite opposite us. When I looked at you, I noticed you were looking at me. Big embarrassment. So we immediately averted our gazes.

Then I thought it was odd to see a girl by herself. I don't think I'd have stayed in the Gardens if Mac and Steve hadn't been there – I don't like being alone. The fact you didn't seem to care made me think something had happened to you. Maybe you'd been thrown over by some bloke, had a row with him. Or maybe you were a junkie waiting for your supplier. You were my age, but you had a look that made me think you might be older. I noticed your long hair and its centre parting, the fact you were wearing a skirt, and your three-quarter-length sheepskin coat, a rather tatty one. It was far too big on you. You were listening to a Walkman too.

It was rude to stare, so I stopped paying you attention. Instead I told Mac and Steve I had some booze with me. I brought out the vodka. The bottle was still over half full. There was a stirring of interest. I passed the vodka between us. I was aware that you were watching us closely now.

"Who's she?" I asked Steve, who was sitting next to me.

"Dunno. She's been there half an hour or so."

You still had your eyes on us. I knew you wanted some of the drink and I couldn't see why I shouldn't offer you some. I didn't feel sorry for you. It wasn't that. I felt that you were one of us, and it would be wrong to leave you out. Also, I wanted to find out what you were doing there. And I wanted to cheer myself up, to forget about what had just happened to me. It was still quite early, just after nine.

I got up and walked over to you.

"D'you want to join us?"

You looked up at me and grinned.

"Yeah, all right, then."

You sat next to me on the bench and I noticed how thin your legs were. So thin that I didn't even feel jealous in the way you always do when you see a girl thinner than you. I wondered for a moment if you were anorexic – there was a girl in our class once who had an eating disorder. Your sheepskin coat stunk. It was musty and old. I passed you the vodka and you took a long, grateful slug from the bottle.

"I'm Cat," I said.

"Jan," you said quickly.

I noticed you held on to the bottle. I didn't mind. Maybe you needed it. I wasn't going to ask you any questions 'cause I knew that could be scary. I just hoped you'd talk. And to my surprise, you did. A lot of it was f-this and f-that, which I wouldn't have thought so much of, if it was coming from a bloke. And don't worry, I won't repeat all your bad language here – it will give totally the wrong impression.

"These your mates?" you asked. Didn't wait for an answer. "They've been here for ages. Don't do much. I've been listening to Queen Latifah. She's top. I'm not saying I don't like blokes doing hip-hop – Dr Dre is cool and that, and I like Snoop, but she's wicked."

Your words came out like machine-gun fire, like your mind was working faster than your mouth. You still hadn't let go of the vodka but I didn't care. I just couldn't work you out. From the outside you looked like you might be homeless or something, or someone from one of those really bad housing estates that are in the local papers all the time. And your voice was coarse and aggressive. But what you were saying struck me as clever, as clever as anything I'd read or heard. So I had to re-assess you. I wanted to keep you talking.

"But what about the violence in rap? A lot of it is against women."

"Yeah, right, I know that." You carried on with the vodka. "But it's like, you don't listen to the words in that way. You listen to the music too. The beat. And it's like, you're one who's rapping. You don't listen and think, this guy would beat me – you think *you're* doing it to someone else? Like you think of someone you hate when you listen to Snoop."

"I suppose I do," I said, interested.

"Here," said Mac. "Pass it along."

Your eyes darted in his direction. I noticed you flinched. Very reluctantly you handed me the bottle. I gave it to Mac and Steve who took some. I had a mouthful myself then passed it back to you. For some weird reason, it felt as if it was yours now.

"Listen," you said. You passed me one of the earpieces of your Walkman and I put it in my ear. We listened to Queen Latifah together. I liked it. It was raw. When Mac and Steve got up to go I didn't mind. I was slightly pissed, I liked you, I liked the music and everything felt cool again.

I wondered then if I could probe a little.

"D'you live round here?" I asked.

"Yeah – not far – with my mate Sally. She's all right."

So you weren't homeless but it sounded as if you'd left home.

"Are you at college or...?"

"No." This briefer answer told me to lay off for a while. I volunteered some information about me. I told you I was at school but it was pissing me off. I thought you'd look down at me for mentioning school – it has to be the saddest word in the English language – but you didn't. You started one of your rants again.

"School? Yeah – crap, isn't it? Except for English. I liked my English teacher. He read us these brilliant poems and then we had to, like, write our own. He said, make up your own rules. A poem has to have rules, he said, but you can make them up. So I used to do these crazy things, like write poems all round the edges of the page, and colour in the rest black or something. And he freaked and said it was good. Really good. And then sometimes he just read us stories. Good stories. There was one, once, about this kid who built a cart or something – no, his Dad did, and then he went down the hill in it and some bus ran him over. It made me cry. Mr Shepherd, he was good at reading. Yeah."

I wondered if you had any GCSEs but it's not a thing you can ask. Even though to everyone I know it feels like such an important thing. By now I was happy to let you have all the vodka. I reckon that was why you had so much to say – you were getting completely leathered. I wondered if you were an alcoholic, only you seemed a bit young to be one. An alkie was an old bloke, reeked of beer, hunted around in bins and staggered around the town centre late at nights, or sat in the Gardens looking wrecked. The vodka was making you higher by the minute.

"I like it here," you said. "They leave you alone here. It's, like, the only bit of town like that. Well, some of them leave you alone. But you meet some right bastards. Your mates seem OK. D'you come here a lot?"

"Yeah, I do," I said.

"I'll see you again, maybe."

"Yeah," I said. "I'd like that." I was telling the truth. I'd found everything you'd said interesting. You were different to Lucy and Fliss and Toni and everyone. It also felt good to have a friend in the Gardens who was female. I got on with Bex OK but it felt kind of superficial. You and me, Jan, we were sitting sharing a Walkman and vodka and it was good.

"I've had a crap evening," I said suddenly.

"Yeah? Why?"

You were genuinely interested. I told you about discovering Taz had a boyfriend, and how stupid I felt not realising. Though you were drunk and getting drunker by the minute, you listened attentively.

"Queers are all right," you said. "It doesn't matter, him being a poof."

Your language shocked me. I only ever used the word 'gay', or 'homosexual' if we were having a discussion in class. But I liked the way you forgave Taz on my behalf. It helped me to begin to forgive him.

I knew it was late now, and that I'd better be getting home. I guessed I should be able to get a taxi easily enough. You'd finished the vodka and I was beginning to worry about you. I thought it would be wrong to leave you completely out of it in the middle of the Gardens. You wouldn't be able to look after yourself.

"Hey, Jan, I've got to go," I said. "Do you want to share a taxi?"

For a minute I thought you were going to say yes. You looked pleased, grateful. Then your mind kind of stumbled like it does when you're pissed.

"No," you said. "I got to be somewhere. But look, do you have any change?"

I got out my purse. I only just had enough for the taxi and I said so, but gave you a couple of 20p pieces I found.

"No, thanks anyway," you said, and gave them back to me, not angrily, but like it wasn't enough. I hesitated. Ought I to give you my taxi money?

"I need the rest to get home," I said guiltily.

"It don't matter," you said. "I'm all right now." You looked far from all right. You were fumbling with your Walkman as you tried to stop the tape and fit everything into your pocket. You hair hung over your face like a curtain so I couldn't see your expression.

"I'm all right now," you said again. "Like, effing brilliant. I'm going to this party. All my mates are there. And my boyfriend who's dead fit and he's got this ring for me, he's gonna ask me to marry him. But I'm late, so I'll see ya, Cat. Thanks for the booze. I'll see you again."

I was scared now as I thought you might be mentally ill. I'd heard my mum going on about care in the community and I knew that lots of mental patients were on the streets. Because that stuff you were saying about a party, it was crap and we both knew it. And I think I would have stopped you if you hadn't got up then and walked away fast, determined, as if you wanted to get away from me.

No, I didn't feel sorry for you. I liked you, plain and simple. I hoped that by hanging round the Gardens I might see you again, like you said. You were someone I could talk to, if I needed. So I left the Gardens and went to hail a taxi.

To Dave (3)

So it was about then I began drinking more regularly. What I mean is, it wasn't just when I went out. There were other times. Secret times.

It helped that my parents were quite heavy drinkers too. But hold on – I'm not blaming them. If there hadn't been drink in the house I would have found some elsewhere. It's not as though it's difficult to get hold of. It was just that having booze in the house simplified matters. There was still loads left from the party, and Dad had been on a trip to Germany and come back with even more. I took a whole bottle of gin and no one noticed it had gone. No one said anything. I reckon Dad thought Mum had drunk it and Mum thought Dad had drunk it. There was a kind of conspiracy of alcohol in the house. If Dad complained about Mum's drinking, she could equally complain about his.

And it was quite easy for me to go into the offie, different ones. My parents were always generous with money. They were proud to be able to give it to me, proud to be able to say that their daughter didn't need to have a

Saturday job – she was free to concentrate on her A-levels. Yes, I know that was a bit of a joke. But providing for their daughter was a big thing with them. And I had a special clothes allowance too; they put thirty quid a month in and I was supposed to buy my shoes, school clothes, stuff like that out of it.

More of a problem was disposing of the bottles. Sometimes I wrapped them up in old supermarket carrier bags and put them in the wheelie bin. Or I'd take them to school and throw them in bins on the way. When I couldn't be bothered – if I was too pissed at night – I put cans in an old rucksack I had and hid it in my wardrobe.

I'd drink beer, but mainly I liked spirits because you could hide them in things and disguise the taste. I kept a bottle of Coke in my bedroom. So some nights I would go to bed early and have something to drink. I'd bought some good music around that time – Queen Latifah. You've not heard of her? She's wicked. I just listened to that and the drink cheered me up.

Or another thing I would do – not every day, though – would be to pour some vodka or gin into a vacuum flask, and take it to school. Around lunchtime I'd go to the toilets and it was easy to slip into a cubicle and have a swig before lessons. It helped me get through the day. OK, so I admit I wasn't just drinking to have fun any more. This was a new stage. But I know you won't judge me. What's so terrible about having a quick drink? Other kids smoked in the toilets and they were risking being caught. I wasn't. And it's wrong to drink and drive – I'd never do that, not ever – but drink and go to Geography lessons – there's no law against it. And when you think about it, there are all these businessmen who go for business lunches – my Dad's one of them – and they drink like fish, then go back to the office and work. I'm seventeen, an adult. So why can't I? It was a bit rank, having to drink in the toilets, but I wasn't keen on my friends knowing. Because they'd have been all concerned and would have split on me to a teacher, saying it was for my own good, which is what people say to justify interfering in your life. It was my choice to drink. I liked it. It helped me. When I drank I formulated all these plans about how I would leave school and get a job to earn some money so I could travel. Or even that I would start working again – tomorrow. Drink does that to you – it makes you feel capable of anything.

So you won't be surprised to hear that I dived into the toilets and had a mega-swig of vodka before the time my parents came in for the Meeting – them, Mrs Dawes, the Head, and me. They were going to sort me out once and for all.

To Mrs Dawes (3)

You were waiting outside the Head's office, shook Mum and Dad's hands, knocked timidly on the Head's thick wooden door, backed off as if alarmed by your own temerity.

"Come in!" boomed his voice.

All that polite business with chairs and the Head and my dad waiting until all the ladies had sat down. The Head had come out from behind his massive desk and was sitting in a little circle with us. There he was, with Dad on his left, Mum, me, and you on his right. You crossed your legs and clasped your hands like a good girl. I just wanted to laugh. It was like we were going to play musical chairs or something. There was this basic incongruity of us all trying to be matey in the Head's study of all places, with those heavy bay windows, his certificates framed on the wall, stacks and stacks of books and reports on education, stifling, headache-making, utterly respectable. And us in a cosy little circle.

Not that I had anything against the Head. He was all right in assemblies and when he was interviewed in the papers. He had a sense of humour, which we all appreciated. People said he did his job well and we found him approachable but a bit scary. You know his daughter was in the year above mine, but she was quiet as a mouse. I suppose you had to be, if you were the Head's daughter. Keep your head down, I was thinking. A joke. Because to tell you the truth, I was beginning to feel slightly hysterical.

"Now, Catherine," he said, affable, relaxed but with a detectable edge, "perhaps we ought to start with you telling us why we're here."

Mum twitching by my side. Everyone looking at me. Sense of not being able to breathe. You shot me a look of solidarity because you would have hated to have been put on the spot like that. Thanks, Mrs Dawes – it made a difference.

"Because I haven't been working," I said. I was quite neutral as if I was talking about somebody else. Which, in a way, I was.

The Head nodded sagely, acknowledging I'd given the correct answer.

"And also to find out why," he added. "And what we can do about it." He liked verbal footnotes.

I felt as if I was being pushed against a wall. I knew you were all trying to help and if it wasn't for the drink I'd had before I came in I'm not sure I could have handled your suffocating concern.

The Head continued.

"Perhaps if you were to describe the problem in your own words..."

"I seem to have lost motivation," I said.

It was easier to talk your language.

"Oh dear, oh dear," said the Head. "You of all people! With eight A-stars at GCSE! Catherine. I'll put it to you straight. You're one of our brightest sixth formers. A credit to the school. Your teachers have absolute faith in you. I have absolute faith in you. The world is your oyster. Do you know, you could study anything you wanted at university? You could be anything you want."

He was only succeeding in terrifying me more. I didn't know what I wanted to be. I hate it when people say that to you, what do you want to be? Expecting you to have your life all mapped out. I was silent.

"Mrs Dawes!" declared the Head, inviting you to continue the pep talk. You were more hesitant.

"It's true, Catherine, as I've often told you. You are a gifted pupil. Maybe if we spent some time in the Careers Office and you found a profession that interested you, that might give you some motivation?"

The Head nodded approvingly as this was just the sort of solution he liked best: practical, putting the school in a good light, achievement-orientated. You looked pleased he approved of you.

"Catherine once wanted to be a barrister," my father

supplied, recalling a brief phase I went through two years ago.

"She also mentioned the civil service," Mum said.

"Well, Catherine?" asked the Head.

"I'm not sure."

"Perhaps Catherine is going through a reassessment of what she wants to do with her life," you said, trying to help me again. "That might be the problem."

At this point the Head intervened. You were doing too well. He had to take some of the credit.

"Yes, I think we're agreed on that, Mrs Dawes. The question is, and I put it to you, what are we going to do about it?"

Dad nodded enthusiastically. He and the Head were carved from the same block.

"Do you think, Catherine," the Head pursued, "you'll be able to take up the pen again in time for the examinations?"

They were three weeks away. Two papers in each of my four AS-levels. I had learned nothing. Three pieces of coursework were incomplete. It was like one of those nightmares you have when you feel paralysed, pinned down, emitting only a tiny squeak when you want to scream for help.

"Because if you can't," the Head continued, glancing at my parents, "there's no shame involved. You can leave school. You're seventeen."

Leave school? Oh, no! That wasn't what I wanted. Not yet, anyhow. I could see what he was doing, putting the frighteners on me. Showing me the alternatives. Bastard. I wondered whether he'd cooked this up with my parents. Panic pricked my arms and forehead.

"I don't want to leave," I said.

"Fair enough," he said.

"Perhaps, Headmaster," you piped up at that moment, "we might give Catherine some extra support. I was thinking of counselling – maybe a professional?"

That was sweet of you though I would never have seen a counsellor in a million years. Your suggestion wasn't too well received.

"I don't think Catherine has *psychological* problems," my mother said frostily. To her, there was a stigma attached to therapy. "If she needs to talk, she always has me." Touché. Mum's a doctor. She knows everything medical.

"No time for a counsellor," the Head said. "Exams in three weeks. It's a challenge, Catherine. Are you up for it?"

"Don't you think," you persisted, "that it's also a case of too much pressure? With the move from three to four subjects at A-level, and the fact that the students know their university applications depend on the AS results. If there was more time…"

You stopped talking, Mrs Dawes, because no one was listening to you. Mum and Dad were waiting to hear my response to the Head. The Head was waiting to hear my response to the Head. I thought, this is all a silly game. None of it is real. It's meaningless. None of you can control me. I don't have to play by your rules, but I do have to survive given that the rules exist. So I decided to make life easy for myself. It was the cleverest thing to do.

"I do want to sit the exams," I said.

In a way, it was true. I reckoned I probably knew enough to get by, even if I didn't do my best. And the easiest thing to do would be to stay at school and take them.

"And will you work, Catherine?" asked the Head.

I could hardly say no. "Yes," I said. "I can see what you're saying. I'll do my best."

"Good, good!" the Head said. "I'm sure Mrs Dawes will help you sort out what needs to be done. I can see you might have to write off some of the outstanding essays. But with two or three hours work a night I should imagine you'd be able to make up a lot of lost ground. Just a blip, eh, Catherine? Just a blip."

The word 'blip' sent me into hysterics. The Head sounded so funny saying it. Blip. What kind of word is that? The last few weeks, my life with Taz, my new friends, my mood swings, a blip. A blip on his radar screen. I could only partly suppress my laughter but luckily it came out as a smile. Everyone thought I was cheering up.

"And I'm sure you'll play your part, Dr and Mr Holmes. Lots of hot chocolate brought up to her room!"

My mother smiled ironically. I knew she resented being told how to do her job. That amused me even more.

"I'd like that, Mum," I said.

You all laughed, thinking the tension had been broken up.

"You see, in the end, Catherine, it's quite easy," said the Head. "Don't think about it, just do it!"

Yes, I thought, that what Hitler's officers did in the Second World War. But I smiled at him and repeated his words. It was fun playing along with everybody.

"Just do it," I said. "I will, I'll do my best. I feel better now. A lot better."

God, it was so easy, acting the good girl. I was surprised I hadn't done it before.

Mum took my hand and squeezed it.

"I think," I continued, "I just let it get on top of me. And all my outstanding work grew to a big thing in my mind. But I think I have a perspective on it now."

"That's my girl," the Head said, smirking.

"I mean, I've never failed an exam in my life and I'm not going to be defeated by these ASs."

"That's the old Catherine speaking!" my dad said.

"I'll draw up a timetable tonight," I said.

"Excellent, excellent."

I was feeling exultant at the success of my deception and slightly sick all at once. Now it was a matter of pretending to work. I hoped I could pull it off. I just needed time. If I sat the exams I could carry on at school till July, and then there would be the holidays anyway. Then I would have a clearer idea about everything, I would know what to do. Maybe I would do well in my exams without any work. Maybe the world would end. Like, who's to say? It was just a matter of surviving one day at a time. Anything I did to survive was OK. Including lying about my intentions.

"Thank you," I said to the Head. "I feel better now. I'm sorry to have been such a trouble."

"Not at all, Cathy," you said.

My mother flinched. She hated anyone calling me Cathy. She said it was common. Catherine was my name.

"It's been very worthwhile," my dad said, getting up, shaking the Head's hand. "Very worthwhile."

I began to wonder whether I could get out on the weekend and go to the Gardens again.

To Taz (6)

For various reasons, I remember George's party very vividly.

It must have been a couple of weeks or so after the night in Satin, and we'd seen each other several times since. In the end, I found it interesting, the stuff about your sexuality. I know I must have been a nuisance, quizzing you about it, asking you when you first thought you might be gay, how could you fancy both sexes, which sex did you prefer, but you didn't seem to mind. You still made me feel I was your best friend.

I didn't exactly stop fancying you, but I was OK with the fact I could never properly have you. I'm not one of those obsessive freaks who moon about over one person and make stuff up in their own mind. The funny thing is, in my experience it's usually blokes who are like that. They're the romantic ones and it's the girls who are more practical, more down to earth. Like, Lucy and Brad. He'd already told her he loved her; she was like, what do you mean by love, and frankly, she was getting a bit scared by it. Someone should have told him to lay off her a bit. Or do you think boys just confuse lust with love?

The answers weren't important. I didn't mind not having a bloke and in some ways it was easier, just being able to act how I wanted, get smashed, not care what people thought, what one particular person thought, and I could see that having you as my special but not boy friend was probably just what I needed. I was still able to tell you the truth, how I went to school every day, sat in lessons, listened sometimes, dreamed other times. Joined in the chat in the common room, made coffee, acted normal. Borrowed essays off people, took them home, rushed through rewrites of them, handed them in. The teachers were encouraging because at least they were getting work in now, even if it wasn't my best. It meant my parents were off my back too. I stayed in my room, read a bit, chilled, and made out I was learning. So I was free to go out.

On the night of George's party we were in the Gardens, at a loose end. Mac had had some weed earlier, but it was finished. We had hardly any cash. We were indecisive, in danger of arguing about what to do next. Then Bex got a text off a mate of hers, saying there was a party at George's. Mac and Steve were laughing, but getting ready to go, no question. I asked you who George was. Some sad old bloke, you said. Buys his friends. You go round to his place and he lays on the booze. Does he fancy you? I asked. You laughed. You said I still wasn't getting the hang of this bisexual thing. You said, come to George's, and you'll see.

Then as we left the Gardens I saw Jan, or rather, she saw me. She looked pleased.

"Hiya," she said. "Are you leaving?"

"We're off to George's place," I said. It was possible she might know George.

"Can I come?"

"Sure," you said. Jan grinned at you and fell into step with us. I felt it was my job to introduce you and I did, saying that I'd met Jan in the Gardens, and she was into rap. I didn't need to say much else. Jan was a high-octane talker.

"Yeah. I bought some albums today. I got some dosh, see. Do you want me to get some booze for the party? I can. I got the dosh. I'm not looking for a free ride. Where are we going? Where does this bloke George live? Have you got any slap, Cat, if it's a party?"

But Jan looked OK. Do you remember her long, dark hair, like in a commercial? And because her skin was pale it made her eyes look big. And with her being so thin, she stood out. I could see you were intrigued by her too.

We must have walked for about half an hour to get to George's. He lived just out of town, along an old Victorian terrace with three-storey houses divided into flats. A bit grotty. Rubbish on the steps, weeds, smell of rotting vegetables from somewhere. He had one of those entryphone things. A bloke loaded with piercings answered the door to us and we all piled in, climbing up two flights of cracked lino-covered stairs. Next to a dirty old toilet with the door open was George's flat.

It was buzzing. Lots of people there, some I recognised from the Gardens. You pointed out George to me. He was a fat bloke who looked in his mid twenties. A fat face, one of those faces that looked like someone had blown it up with a bicycle pump. Little slitty eyes creased into a smile. He wore trousers that were way too small for him, so his gut hung out over the waistband. Did he think that looked cool? He was glistening with sweat, but was pleased to see us, even though he didn't seem to know who we were. He welcomed us in, pointed out the tiny kitchen where the booze was. He didn't need to do that twice.

There were cans and cans of lager and beer. We helped ourselves and drank straight from the cans. I was curious.

"Who *is* George?" I asked you again.

"Don't know exactly. He's spoken to us a few times. He goes into Bex's café. He's got no mates. He works in the warehouse at the brewery. He has these parties, for the company."

I looked around. I supposed that was OK, throwing parties to make friends – didn't everyone do it? Only the weird thing about this party was that everyone looked about ten years younger than George. It was the kids he'd invited. I wondered if he was a paedophile, but somehow

I didn't think so. The people he'd invited, they were just the street crowd and they were exploiting him. They weren't vulnerable, innocent kids. Hell, they were Mac and Steve and Taz and Bex and me. George stood by, just grinning, watching everybody. He was just getting off on being part of a crowd. He was willing to rent the crowd. Like extras in a film.

His flat was cheap, nothing special. There was a fireplace with a gas fire, an old telly, two tatty two-seater settees with scratchy covers. But you couldn't really see the flat for the people standing around drinking. He'd turned the radio on loud and there was dance music banging out. The nearer we stood to the kitchen, the less the music interfered with the conversation.

"Look," said Jan. She pushed up the sleeve of the jacket she was wearing and showed me a watch. It had a thick pink strap and a bubble-shaped face.

"Cool," I said.

"Yeah," she said. "Got it today."

"Is it your birthday or something?"

"Yeah!" she said. "No, not really. I wanna dance."

And she did. She took off her jacket, threw it in a corner, moved into the centre of the room and began to shuffle around to the music, attracting some attention. She didn't care about the attention. She was just getting into the music. She was swinging her hair around, more and more, until it seemed to have a life of its own. You asked me again, Taz, who she was. I told you I didn't really know. We watched her together. She was wearing a T-shirt that was too small for her and showed up the fact she wasn't wearing a bra. Not that she needed to. She was quite small. Her skirt was short but she could take it. She had good legs.

After a while she came back to us. You gave her the can you were drinking and went into the kitchen to get another. You started talking to someone there, leaving Jan and me alone. She slithered to the floor, her back against the wall. I got down and joined her.

"You really freaked out," I said.

"Yeah. I like a good bop. I'm all hot now, sweating like a pig." She drank greedily from her can.

"Shit!" she said, and crawled along the floor for her jacket, found it, and began rooting through the pockets. Her face relaxed. "Still there," she said. She put the jacket over her lap.

"What did you think you'd lost?" I asked her.

"My money," she said. "I owe some of it to Sally. She's my mate. I live with her. Her and her daughter. She's got this baby daughter, Kayla. So I have to help with the food and rent. Or I baby-sit. She screams like hell but she stops after a while. She has these tantrums, see. And she gets ratty when Sally has to go out. So it's good for her, having me there. It's dead good, this watch, isn't it?"

Jan admired it again. It was all right but it looked quite cheap.

"Shall I tell you how I got it?"

She wanted to, so I encouraged her.

"From the covered market. When they weren't looking. They'd left them out on the stall while some customer was giving them grief about a handbag that was wrong or something. I took the lot. I flogged some. I kept this one."

OK, Taz, I'll be honest. That kind of shocked me. Only at first. Because I'd never been tempted to steal, but then I thought, hey, what kind of prig was I? I nicked booze off my parents and if they didn't give me money, who knows what I'd do? And my dad spends ages with his accountant finding ways of minimising his tax bill. And my mum accepts all these freebies from the drug company reps that visit her. People are always taking things off other people. And looking at Jan, I reckoned she needed the money. So I decided it was OK. Every time I do that, break through a taboo, decide something is all right that I thought wasn't, I get a thrill. A dark, electric thrill.

I showed Jan I didn't mind by admiring her watch, even though it wasn't my thing.

"I know these guys," Jan went on, "who can get rid of stuff for you. And get you stuff. Do you know them? Ali and Jono?"

"No," I said.

Jan snuggled down by the wall.

"This is cool," she said. "I like you, Cat. You're my mate, right?"

"Right," I said.

"Sally is my mate too, but she's older than me. She kind of looks after me. So it's different. When she's not working, she's, like, exhausted, just watches telly and sleeps. Or hangs around in the flat. I like going out. I don't want to end up like Sally, stuck with a kid in a flat. That's not gonna be me, no way."

"What are you going to do?" I asked her.

"Me? Right. I'm gonna get a band and write my own stuff and perform it. And I'll get to be on the box, and dead famous and rich. Then someone, a DJ or someone else in the business, he'll fall in love with me and we'll get married. It'll be in all the papers. So then I won't have to work no more and live in this mansion in the country. We'll share this big bedroom with a four-poster bed. All romantic with flowers everywhere. And Sally and Kayla will move there and do all the housework. I'll have four kids, two of each. Adam, Zak, Bella and Rosy."

"You've got it all worked out," I said.

"Yeah. What are you going to be?"

I shrugged, feeling uncomfortable. "Don't know, yet."

Jan looked surprised, as if everyone ought to know where they were heading. But really I didn't have a clue. Still don't.

"I'm having an ace time," Jan said, pushing her hair behind her ears.

The party was noisier than ever now. Not the music, but people shouting to be heard. The atmosphere was like a very busy pub before closing time, the air thick with smoke and a desperation to have a good time. That was something everyone wants – to have a good time. Maybe that was the answer. What did I want to be? Someone who has a good time. But George wanted friends. The ironic thing was that though it was his party he was still on the edge of things, can in hand. Jan wanted it all: fame, riches, a family. Something occurred to me then, and since we were officially friends now, I felt I could ask her.

"Do you have a family?" I asked.

"Yeah, once," she said. "Don't remind me."

"So you're not in touch with them, " I said carefully.

She scowled, stubbed out the cigarette she was smoking. I stopped my questions.

"Families are the pits," I said. "I can't stand mine."

"Me neither," she said, cheering up. "Let's dance."

By that time I'd drunk enough not to care what people thought of me, so Jan and I stood up and began to go manic, freaking out to the music. It was brilliant. She was mad, and because she was so mad, it was like she was daring me to go further. People were cheering us on. Normally I hate being the centre of attention, but I didn't care that night. There was more than enough beer. We drank, we danced, we shouted to the music. Incredible sense of being completely alive at that moment, careless, carefree, whirling, mad. Me and Jan.

In the end we were exhausted. We both joined you again. I wrote my number on a piece of paper you gave me and put it in a side pocket in Jan's skirt. She told me she didn't have a phone.

"Where do you live?" I asked her.

"Behind the Save garage, by the chippie."

"Where's that?"

Perhaps she was just about to explain – I really don't know. You were there – what do you think? What happened next was that some more people came into George's flat. Older blokes, more his age, some older. I sensed they were looking at us. Because of all the wild dancing we'd done, I'd sobered up a bit. I didn't like the way they were staring.

"Bloody hell," one of them said. "It's Mary."

Jan clutched hold of my arm. I noticed her fingernails were bitten to the quick.

"I gotta go," she said.

So I took her by the hand, and avoiding the men we got out of the flat and ran down the stairs. You followed, remember?

Once outside and sure they weren't following, Jan stopped, casting anxious glances back at the flat.

"Who were those blokes?" I asked.

"My jacket!" she screamed.

You went back to get it, Taz. Then Jan came over really weird. She said she couldn't wait, she'd ring me about the jacket. She didn't live far. She had to go. I could see there was no way I could restrain her. By the time you returned she'd gone, leaving us with an old denim jacket. Curious, I looked in the pockets. There was thirty quid in there. I swore.

"I'll keep it for her," I said. You nodded.

I checked the other pockets. There was a pack of ciggies and some matches, crumpled tissues, an old chocolate wrapper, some copper coins and a jar of strawberry lip balm.

We walked around for a bit, discussing Jan. We got a night bus back to my place and you walked me home. When I got ready for bed that night I realised something was missing. My purse had gone. With my school library card and about seven quid. Either I'd dropped it or someone had taken it. It could have been anyone at the party, or Jan. I kind of hoped it was Jan. I wouldn't have minded her having the money. Not one little bit.

To the Examiner

To what extent does his ability to exploit good fortune and weak opposition explain Bismarck's success in unifying Germany by 1871?

*[*Do **not** attempt this question if you have answered Question **2**]*

I don't know.

Well, that's my answer. And it's right. I really don't know *anything* about Bismarck. He's not even on my syllabus but I decided to answer this question because since I haven't done any revision at all I might as well answer this. Also, I can't sit here just staring into space. I need to write *something*. I've decided to write to you, to give you a break. So put down your pen and read.

There are the invigilators, thinking everything is running like clockwork, and they haven't got a clue I've opted out of European History.

Perhaps I should at least *attempt* the question. *To what extent does his ability...?* Answer: to a great extent. If that's the right answer, will you give me a mark just for guessing right? 1 out of 25, rather than 0? Because exams are about luck as well as how much you know, stuff like whether the right questions come up. But not only luck. Some people are just good at exams, they can memorise masses of stuff. There's Daniel Hill sitting in front of me scribbling away. He has a photographic memory but he's a racist. He calls the Asian boys in our class shitfaces. You've probably already marked his script as his will be on top of mine, but when you've given him an A, just remember what I said. I challenge you to put him down a grade or two. I think a racist is a bad historian by definition. That's what I've learnt by studying History.

Back to Bismarck. No. Perhaps not. Exams are also unfair to the people who panic. Antonia Lewis – you'll come to her script shortly – is just a bundle of nerves. She spends half an hour before exams in the loo. She was white as a sheet this morning. Then when she sees the paper she always chooses the wrong question – by accident, not deliberately, like me – and spends far too long on the first one and rushes the rest. She can be a bit ditsy at times but she's a nice girl and is our Form Charity Rep. Go on – push her up a few marks.

But you won't, because exams are a serious business. I wonder how much you get paid per script? Do you ever worry that you are controlling someone's destiny? The difference between an A or a B, or a B and a C, could end someone's career. Or are you sitting there with a red pen and a gin and tonic? God – I could do with one right now.

You think I'm joking. I'm not. I've got into the habit of drinking lately. It's a way of dealing with stuff. It makes reality fuzzy and softens the edges of things. I expect Bismarck drank too. If he was a German I daresay he drank beer and ate sausages. Did he wear those funny leather shorts that you see some Germans wearing? But don't think I'm an alcoholic or that I drink every day. Just most days. I have to be careful because I don't particularly want my parents to find out. They'll give me grief. Do you have kids? Do they take exams? I'm curious now. I'm getting interested in you. Has any other candidate ever written you a letter like this before?

Actually, it's quite therapeutic, as well as being a necessary disguise. You see, I haven't done any revision at all. That's because I wanted to stay at school at least till the summer. I wanted to play for time. So I reckon I can sit these exams – turn up for each exam and write – and only when the results come through in August will I have to deal with this mess. August is a long time away. A lot can happen in that time. Though God knows what.

Maybe I'll decide what I want to do with my life. The problem is that I've lost enthusiasm for everything except going out, being with people, getting out of it. And I can't think of one good reason why that shouldn't be enough.

OK – I admit it's good to help people, and I admire nurses and aid workers and that – but I couldn't do that. Most people I know only do good stuff so other people admire them, or they like that smug glow they get when they buy a Big Issue. Look! I'm helping the homeless! Look at me, everybody!

I can't see the point of exams. You get qualifications, labels. But they don't open doors – they do the opposite. They *rob* you of choices. Once you've got a degree you can't go and work at McDonalds or on the tills at Tesco. If you did, people would think you were a failure, even if you'd made the rational decision to have an undemanding job. You might want an undemanding job. You might be sick to death of marking exam scripts. Maybe you're even enjoying reading this rubbish.

Money corrupts. Power corrupts – do I get a mark for that? Civilisation is all about pretending – pretending to be polite, proper, civil when really you just want to act like the animal you are. I'm not saying civilisation is a bad thing, but that it's imposed on people – it isn't natural. Like, civilised people go to war, don't they?

I'm sorry, I'm getting confused.

I'm thinking, what if I leave home? I could probably get a job in a café or shop, and if I shared a place, maybe I could afford the rent. I could try being independent. I have a friend called Jan who lives in a flat – maybe there would be room for me. She lives with an older woman and her daughter, which is a bit of a problem... Maybe Jan could leave and we could flatshare. That would be awesome. I'd like that, cooking our own meals, inviting people round. And it would give me time to think about what next.

Or I could just leave school and re-enrol at college, where Taz is. He doesn't get as much hassle as me. You will have realised this centre is an independent fee-paying school. That's why the scripts are so good. The teachers spoon-feed us because the parents want their money's worth. The candidates can't wait to forget everything they've learnt as soon as they walk out of the examination room. Hardly any of them are really interested in History. Doesn't that make you sad?

Or I could go and be a voluntary worker somewhere like India or Africa. That's not a bad idea. It would be a long way away from my parents. But don't go thinking I've got terrible parents or anything. You're not reading a tale of child abuse or a rancorous divorce. My mum is a doctor and my father a company secretary. They're good, caring people. They love me. They mean well. And they want me to *be* them.

Tough.

Being an historian, I bet you're the analytical type. Don't try to analyse these ramblings. Or stick a label on me. I'm not depressed, I'm not a victim but I have X-ray vision. It isn't easy being a superhero.

When I was a little girl I thought it was silly to take risks. I couldn't understand why grown-ups smoked, or worse, took *drugs*! I would never take drugs! Have sex! Get drunk! I would always work hard and be a credit to my parents. But now I've discovered that taking risks creates energy. Your head fills with light; there's this incredible sense that you've created the possibility that anything might happen. That you're experimenting, like a mad scientist. And you might discover the elixir of life, whatever that is.

You still have half a set of scripts to mark. I need only sit here for another half an hour or so. Then after school I'm walking into town to meet Taz for some coffee. He's got to spend all day doing his art. Then we'll go out someplace as I don't have school tomorrow. I'll be looking out for Jan, that friend of mine I told you about. I have her jacket – she left it with me. There was thirty quid in the pocket, which I've kept for her. She had my phone number, but she hasn't rung. I hope she's OK. Half of me thinks she can look after herself, but the other half doesn't. Taz said not to worry – we know she isn't alone as she lives with Sally. But I can't imagine that she would want to leave thirty quid with me. She's poor. I know that. I have evidence, but I'm not going to tell you even though you don't know who she is.

Worrying about Jan stops me worrying about myself, and I think it's better to worry about other people.

Are you having a holiday this summer? I'm not. My parents want to rent a villa in the Dordogne but I've refused to go with them. They say they can't leave me at home by myself. I told them seventeen is well old enough. They said, the expression is 'quite old enough', not 'well old enough'. A bit of a stalemate there.

It's hot in the exam hall. They turned off the fan because it makes a whirring noise and distracts everyone. Daniel Hill keeps asking for more paper. Mrs Dawes is invigilating and she's scurrying towards him, a sheaf of paper in her hand. He barely acknowledges her presence as she carefully places two sheets of paper next to the card with his candidate number. Somebody ought to tell Mrs Dawes not to wear just-below-your-knee-length skirts. They're well unflattering. She must have been sunbathing as her arms below the sleeves of her blouse are red and blotchy. So is the area beneath her neck.

I go golden brown in the sun. Do you? I'm writing this rubbish because if I stop too soon, they'll know something is wrong. So you are in a conspiracy with me. My confederate. My confidant. My buddy. Promise me you won't contact the school about all this. I really don't mind failing this paper – hell, I *want* to. I want to see what it's like to fail – then I'll know the meaning of success.

I feel we've got quite close this afternoon. You're not a

stranger any more. Nor am I, I hope. It's been a relief to get all my thoughts down on paper to a stranger. I ought to do this more often. Perhaps if you give me your address we can correspond. Only joking.

I'm running out of things to say. Help.

The Grand old Duke of York
He had ten thousand men
He marched them up to the top of the hill
Then he marched them—

Mrs Dawes says there's five minutes to go. Phew. Thank you for reading this. Don't feel bad about failing me, like I said. All the best for the future,

Catherine Margaret Holmes.

To Lucy (3)

This is my version of our argument and I hope you'll accept it as an apology. I think it would be a shame if we weren't ever friends again.

It was just after the European History exam. You came out dishevelled, looking exhausted.

"That was really solid," you said. "Did you do the question on Nazi Germany? Or Russia? Did you put in about Rasputin?"

You always liked to dissect the paper afterwards to make sure you were right, that you'd put down what everyone else had. I had reasons of my own for not wanting to discuss the paper. I let you witter on. It was French in the afternoon so neither of us had an exam. I wondered if you were going over to the canteen for lunch or were just going to stay in the common room and eat sandwiches.

"This exam's done my head in," you said. "I wasn't able to revise properly because I've got problems with Brad."

"Problems? I thought he was really into you?"

"Yeah, but—"

Our conversation was cut short. As we entered the common room we saw there was something big going on. There was a crowd in the corner by the coffee machine and just about everybody else who was in the common room was looking over there. There was someone in the middle of the crowd sobbing. We glanced at each other, both mystified. Only it was impossible not to be a ghoul in a situation like that, so we wandered over.

It was Melissa in the middle of the crowd, Melissa sobbing. She looked genuinely distraught. As much as I loathe her, I couldn't help feeling sorry for her. Maybe someone had died or something. Maybe she was having an exam panic. I nudged Fliss and asked her what the problem was. Fliss turned to us, glad to able to do her part in relaying the news.

"Last night Melissa's car was broken into. While she was in it! She was at the lights, just waiting for them to change, and there was like a big explosion and someone had thrown a brick through her window, and took her bag and she had *everything* in it. Her purse, her mobile, her make-up. It was awful."

I admit, it sounded horrific. Once we'd come home and someone had tried to break in while we were out but the alarm frightened him off. That was spooky enough.

"But why is she crying *now*?" I asked Fliss.

Fliss's tone was hushed, deferential.

"Well, she didn't sleep at all last night, the police came round and everything. And they said it was unlikely she'd see her bag again. And she had this new phone, a silver Motorola Wings with her initials engraved, and over a hundred people in her address book, and she's lost all their numbers. And she's got her French exam now, and she came in early to tell the Head of Sixth, and, like, re-living it all has brought it all back."

It was mean of me to think that perhaps Melissa was milking it. By now I reckoned she should have come round. It occurred to me that maybe she was acting up so if she did badly in her French there would be an excuse. Then I hated myself for being so uncharitable. How would I have liked to have been in Melissa's predicament? It was odd how, even though she was such a vile person, so up herself and mean to other people, I still kind of felt sorry for her. I mean, I would have preferred this not to have happened to her. So there must be some good in me. But not a lot, because despite that, I still reckoned she was enjoying the attention. Girls were scurrying around, bringing her drinks, tissues, trying to cheer her up, telling her that her parents would buy her another phone, and hey, what a brilliant opportunity to get a whole new set of make-up!

You pushed through the crowd, didn't you, Lucy? You paid your respects. You knelt by her and held her hand.

She looked at you in mournful gratitude. Poseur, I thought, and again hated myself for my reaction. I was becoming all twisted and cynical. Some of Mel's friends were saying school should let her sit the French exam tomorrow instead. That it was mean of the Head of Sixth to make her do the paper today. Didn't the idiots realise it was an external paper and couldn't be shifted?

It made me want to throw up, the way all the girls were secretly revelling in Melissa's disaster. It was like they fed off tragedy. It gave them all a chance to get maternal and show how loving and caring they all were. Scoring niceness points. It was such a girlie thing to do. The boys just stood around looking awkward. Brad was there, waiting to talk to you.

In the end I decided to leave the crowd. I wasn't wanted. I had some crisps in my school bag and helped myself to those. I sat on one of the armchairs by the window looking over the playground. The common room itself used to be a music room, but then the school filled it with easy chairs and coffee tables and gave it to the sixth form. It still felt like an old classroom, and its makeover sat as uncomfortably on it as a pinny on my Dad. The easy chairs were old, anyway, and there was a rumour that they were infested with fleas or something. They were certainly manky enough.

To be honest, I don't know why I wanted to stay at school. Looking round the common room then I thought it was the place I least wanted to be in the world. But it was familiar. It had in it all the people I knew, who I'd grown up with. They drove me mad at times, but I couldn't imagine being without them. School was the pits, but pits were hidden away and comfortable and hard to get up and out of. Not being at school was hard to imagine. Like not being part of your family.

One of the teachers came in then and spirited Melissa away. The group surrounding her broke up. Brad went up to you and you had a few words with him, then made your way over to me. He left the common room.

"Oh, God," you said. "Oh, God. I wish I knew what to do."

I offered you a crisp. You shook your head. You said you couldn't eat. I encouraged you to tell me what the problem was. I was kind of curious.

"I wish I knew," you said. "I *think* I feel the same way about him, but it's like, he's always there and there's no magic any more. Yeah, the magic has gone."

"Was there magic before?" I prompted.

"In the beginning, before I was sure he really liked me, and when we were first going out. But now – oh, I don't know. He rings me every night and then when everyone went clubbing last Saturday he didn't want to go and I ended up round at his place watching TV with his family and it was like, everybody else was having a good time, and you know…"

"You mean you wanted to go out without him?"

"No! Well, yeah, but not to get off with anyone."

"You're finding him boring?"

"No! We know each other really well. I know what he's thinking sometimes. We're so close, closer than I've been with anyone. Like we're married or something. Like an old married couple."

I pulled a face. "So you want to dump him?"

"No!" you said again. "I can't imagine not going out with him. But, Cath, is it normal to fancy someone else while you're going out with another person?"

"I should guess so. Otherwise so many marriages wouldn't end in divorce."

"Did you fancy anyone else when you were going out with Taz?"

"No."

"Say you did!"

"Why? To make you feel better?" I know I was being ratty but I had one of those black moods coming over me. Partly because of the exam we'd just had, partly because I hated myself because of my mixed reaction to Melissa, partly because I didn't feel like playing the role of counsellor just then. And partly because I needed a drink and you wouldn't leave me alone. I couldn't think how to get to the toilets and leave you.

"You know Nick Ingram in the Upper Sixth? I was talking to him at the bus stop. He's cute. But I shouldn't be thinking like that, should I?"

"You can think what you like."

"But if my feelings were strong enough for Brad, I wouldn't notice other guys. I'd be like, totally into him. And then my mum says I should be playing the field at my age, I'm too young to have a steady boyfriend."

"Playing the field?" I questioned. "It's not a blood sport."

You looked at me weirdly. I felt mean, though there was no reason why I shouldn't be mean. Why do people have to be so bloody nice to each other all the time? Especially girls. I thought you needed a reality dose. It was clear to me you and Brad were past your sell-by date. And that you were using me as a sounding board, or as someone to give you permission to dump him. And I was measuring with my eyes the distance between where we were sitting and the door, from which I could quickly exit to the toilets.

"Only if I finished with him it would break his heart. And Nick Ingram – like, if I was single, would he ask me out? That wouldn't be why I was dumping Brad, though – but if he didn't ask me out… But maybe he's talking to me because I am going out with someone and I'm safe. But I love Brad – it's not just physical, it's deeper that that. He wants us to go on holiday together. Which might be cool, only it's with his parents. Which would be sad, don't you think? Oh, God, why is life so difficult? Like, first I was desperate for a boyfriend and now there are all these possibilities."

"I know what you could do with," I interrupted. "A drink."

"Too right," you said.

"I'm serious," I replied. "Do you fancy one right now?"

"What? You mean go down the pub? But what if a teacher sees us? That happened to Shelley and Rachel. They were in the Wellington and the whole of the Maths department walked in."

"No. I've got some stuff with me."

You looked baffled.

"Come here."

You followed me, curious. I took my bag and we went to the sixth form girls' toilets. Luckily no one was around. Stink of perfume and stale cigarette smoke. Smears on the mirrors. Peeling plaster. I took out my flask, unscrewed the top.

"Vodka," I said. I gulped some down. "Here. Help yourself."

But you didn't. Your forehead creased in puzzlement. Then you began to piece things together, assemble the jigsaw.

"I've seen you with that flask before," you said. "But I just thought it was coffee."

"Yeah, right." I laughed.

"Cath," you said slowly. "You shouldn't be bringing alcohol into school."

I raised my eyebrows at you being such a prig.

"No," you persisted. "You'll get caught. But it's not just that."

"What is it, then?" I challenged you.

"You've not been drunk in school, have you?"

I staggered around the toilets, playing the fool.

"Cath, be serious! Like, it sounds as if you have a problem!"

A *problem*! Here we go again. Girls getting off on other girls' problems. Next thing you'd be going to see Mrs Dawes, telling all our mates. *Cath's got a drink problem! What shall we do? Shall we take her to Alcoholics Anonymous? Poor Cath! I feel so sorry for her!*

"No, Lucy," I said. "No – you're the one with the problem."

"Listen to yourself! You never used to be like that. You used to be so nice, so sweet. You've changed, you know. And I thought it was Taz and all those moshers you've been hanging out with. But now I can see it isn't. You've been drinking secretly. It's affecting your character."

"It's not the bloody drink," I said, furious. "I've bloody grown up. Unlike some people I could mention." I was vicious, defensive.

"What are you saying?" you asked, trembling. I could see I'd really upset you. You were close to tears – no, I think you actually did cry. Only I can't say for sure because I was blinded by a red film of anger. How dare you interfere with my drinking, with my life, making out as if you were so much cleverer than me? You seemed just like my parents or the teachers.

"I'm saying just get off my back, Lucy. Don't meddle with what you can't understand."

"I can't believe you're saying this!"

"You'd better believe it," I said. "Just piss off, will you!"

You left the toilets in floods of tears.

I stood there paralysed. I couldn't believe what I'd just done. I'd dissed you, I'd sworn at you. Believe me – I didn't hate you really – we'd been best friends for so long. I felt like a vandal. Like one of the blokes who had smashed the window of Melissa's car, an emotional thug. Me, of all people. It was like my passion for destroying things was getting the better of me. Or that I didn't know what it was I really wanted to destroy so I chose you, because you were near at hand and a soft target. Or was it the drink? Deep down, I didn't think it was. The mood came first; the drink was a way of coping. Or was it?

I felt like crying now, only crying was weak. I felt sick, light-headed. I went into one of the cubicles. Then I did cry, big silent sobs. I banged my head against the wall. I felt like hurting myself. I understood then why some people went in for self-harm. I couldn't bear to think of what I had just done. You see, I hated myself much more than I hated you.

I did text you an apology but you never replied. Brad said you needed time. Maybe if term hadn't ended so soon we would have had to make friends. I never meant to hurt you. But now in the light of all that happened afterwards, you might be able to forgive me.

Please.

To Dave (4)

It was because I'd fallen out with Lucy I decided to try to trace Jan.

Not immediately. The summer was making me feel lethargic – I mean, lazy, like crashing out all the time. Maybe it was the effect of the exams, the heat, I don't know. I found it hard to get up in the mornings, all too easy to fall asleep at night. I only came awake late, in the Gardens. Out there, even on the hottest nights there was a slight breeze, a reminder that summer wasn't going to last forever.

Most of the time, during those long, muggy summer days, I didn't want to do anything. I was overcome by complete inertia. My mother wondered whether I might have ME or glandular fever after all. I was happy for her to think that. Yeah, I was still drinking. Maybe the drink was responsible – I don't think so. It might have been responsible for me feeling so wretched in the mornings, thick head, heavy limbs. Whatever. Or maybe I found it hard to move because I wanted time to stand still. In August, when my results came through, a bomb would explode. Only I knew I had failed everything. Yeah, a bomb! Even now a Cruise missile is winging its way through the stratosphere ready to wreak total destruction in my life. I'm laughing, but I'm not joking.

So term ended. I slept more than ever. My mother dosed me on St John's Wort which is supposed to be for depression. I took double the dose in case they really were uppers, but they didn't do much. I bought some new clothes with some money I was given, put the rest aside for booze. I don't remember much except being bored. And lonely. I kept thinking about Jan. I still had her jacket and hadn't spent her money. I remember her saying she lived behind the Save garage, by the chippie. I know she was about to be more precise, but then we were interrupted. It occurred to me I ought to be able to find her – there can't be that many Save garages and chippies. I said that to Taz. He reckoned I was right. One night we talked it through. He thought I should look in the telephone directory under Save garages and ask whoever answered the phone if there was a chippie nearby, and if there was, we could go down and check it out. Except he might not be able to come with me because he was working – he'd got a summer job at Next and they were coming up to the sales.

In fact, I wasn't bothered if he came or not. Or to be brutally honest, I felt like doing this myself. Jan was my friend. So one afternoon when I had the house to myself

I did just what Taz suggested. First couple of garages, the people who answered the phone sounded a bit clueless. The third guy gave me directions to a chippie about half a mile away. The fourth said, yeah, there was a chippie just behind them. I felt sure that was the one. I didn't bother to ring the other two garages. I felt quite excited – at last there was something I felt like doing. I was going to find Jan. I put her jacket in an old Sainsbury's bag and her money in my new purse. In a few moments I was out of the house.

Of course I realised that I didn't have an address. But I reckoned that the chippie might be open and if I described Jan they might know her. It was a chance worth taking. I felt in a better mood, lighter, happier. I sent Taz a text message telling him what I was up to from the top of the bus.

The bus stopped just before the garage, which was at a crossroads. The main road was the one I'd just come along. The intersecting road was smaller and had some shops along it. I reckoned it was the intersecting road that I should be going for. I began to walk down it looking for a chippie. There was the Happy Valley Chinese takeaway, and I wondered if that was what Jan meant. But only for a moment. Because on the corner of a road running parallel to the main road was a chippie, an English chippie. The Fryer Tuck. I knew I'd got the right place. But just as I was beginning to feel exultant

I realised that one thing had not gone according to plan. The chippie was closed. I wandered over to it. The notice said that the proprietors were taking their annual holiday and the shop would be closed for two weeks.

So there I was, a stone's throw from Jan, and no clue at all as to where she might live. It even occurred to me she might not even be living there any more. I fought a growing sense of anticlimax, of foolishness. I looked down the street where I was sure Jan lived. It was pretty rank. Red-brick terraced house jammed together, no front gardens, dustbins waiting to be emptied, washing hanging out on lines stretched across the tarmac – I thought there weren't places like that any more. No one was about. I decided to walk along the road – Maple Street – while I debated what to do next. I glanced in at the houses as I did so. One or two were unoccupied – I wondered then if Jan lived in a squat. Others had lace curtains in the windows, probably put up by old people intent on guarding their privacy. Others where you could see into the front rooms looked pretty bare. I reached the end of the street and came to a general store which also said it was an off-licence. So I walked in and bought some cans of beer. The lady who served me was short, plump, wearing a sari and head scarf. I described Jan to her and asked if she knew anyone answering to her description. I don't think her English was very good. She seemed baffled by what I was saying. It made me feel as if I was being weird, as if it was me talking in an incomprehensible language.

So I went back out on the street. There were a couple of kids there now kicking a ball around, and a tabby cat licking itself in the gutter, totally unconcerned. I wished I had the courage to knock on a few doors, but that would have been rude.

Just then a door on the opposite side of the road opened and someone came out – a woman in her late twenties or thereabouts, carefully angling the buggy she was pushing so she could get it over the front step. It was one of those baby buggies with a rack underneath for you to put your shopping on. The woman had dyed blonde hair with the roots showing and I remember thinking she was a bit on the fat side. The baby too – it was one of those babies that looked like it was never going to turn into a toddler but would just get bigger and bigger as a baby, rounder and fatter. It had a dull stare.

Then my mind clicked into gear. Sally and Kayla. Could it be? Only one way to find out. I went up to them.

"Excuse me," I said. "I wonder if you could help me. I'm looking for someone called Jan."

The woman gave me a funny look.

"Are you Sally?" I asked.

"Yeah," she said, a bit suspicious. She had a thick local accent.

"She told me about you," I carried on. "That's your baby Kayla. You see, I'm a friend of Jan's. I met her in Victoria Gardens. She went with me to a party and left her jacket. I've got it." I opened the Sainsbury's bag and showed her. "I just want to return it to her."

I could see Sally weighing me up.

"She's in now," she said. "Why don't you knock on?"

"Yeah. Thanks. Cheers!"

Success! Sally carried on down the street with the baby. I was feeling lucky. I rapped at the door from which Sally had come. Rapped hard. And sure enough in a moment or two the door opened and there was Jan, still in a dressing gown, bare legs, hair a bit awry, but Jan all right. It took her a moment to place me, but when she did she grinned fit to burst.

"Cat! I lost your number!"

"I thought you might have done," I said, grinning too.

"Oh, wicked! Come in!"

I did so. I was really pleased to see her. I hardly noticed the house, just a vague impression that it was a tip, baby stuff everywhere on the carpet, TV playing, yukky baby smell. A white cuddly toy like a polar bear with stains on it.

First off, I gave her her jacket, and then the money. She was really pleased to see it and seemed surprised I hadn't spent it.

"It was yours," I told her. She handled the three notes

lovingly. Then she picked up the remote and muted the TV.

"Can you stay a bit?" I nodded. "Cool! Look, I'll just go and change. I'll get you something to eat. I was going to have lunch." She seemed excited and ran to what I guessed was her bedroom. Now I looked round the tiny room and had to admit it was a bit squalid. The carpet was threadbare and I saw a used nappy or two. I felt sorry for Jan then. There was an open jar of baby dessert with a blue plastic spoon sticking out of it. But loads of toys, enough to start a nursery. Mainly soft toys, teddies, bunny rabbits, floppy dolls.

Jan came back, having put on some shorts and a T-shirt. Her feet were bare.

"I'll make some toast," she said.

The kitchen was at the back. She disappeared into it and before too long came back with rounds of toast and a big bowl of cornflakes for herself.

"I'm starved," she said. "But how did you know where I lived?"

I explained, and she was impressed.

"You're dead clever," she said.

"I haven't seen you in the Gardens lately."

"Yeah. I been busy. But I've been meaning to go. It's ace to see you."

It delighted me that she was so happy to have my company. I felt wanted. It made up for having lost contact with Lucy. Only I also felt slightly uneasy. Seeing Jan at home like this pointed out to me the gulf between us, even though I knew it was only a matter of money. Still, I wasn't used to houses like this, to a mess like this. Then I remembered the beer.

"I brought this," I said, and brought out the cans of Carlsberg. Her face lit up. I gave her one and we began to drink. As I did so I relaxed more. I realised it was more comfortable in a way, a house like this, than the mausoleum that my parents lived in. Like, it didn't matter if you made a mess because there was one already. You could drink beer from the can and feel at ease. Then Jan asked me how I'd been. I told her about school being over for the summer, about my row with Lucy.

"Yeah," she said. "I can't be doing with people fussing about me, either."

"Interfering," I said.

"Yeah."

We were sitting on the floor, our backs to the settee. Dead comfortable. We chatted about Taz for a while – Jan said she liked him. Then Jan said she'd bought these curling-tong things and was going to curl her hair. I said I didn't think she needed to – I really liked her hair as it was. But she said she just wanted a change. She said I could help her this afternoon as Sally had taken Kayla to the clinic and would be ages. I felt happy. It was a long time since I'd just messed with someone, doing girlie things. It amazed me how well me and Jan got on. It was like we'd known each other for ever. She said, why didn't we nick some of Sally's nail varnish and paint our toenails? Cool, I said. She couldn't do her fingernails as they were bitten right down. She said she was good at nail painting, she did designs. So she put some music on, I took off my sandals and carefully she put on a base coat of black. I giggled – it tickled. She was chatting away.

"Kayla's had this cough and Sally's worried about it. But they'll know at the clinic. It's been keeping her up at night. But it doesn't bother me. I sleep down here on the sofa."

"Is there only one bedroom?" I asked.

"Yeah. But I like it down here 'cause I can watch telly late. I watch the discussions sometimes. I like to know what's going on, the news and that."

She sat back and waited while the black varnish dried.

"Can we go out tonight, Cat?" she asked.

"Hey, yeah!" I said. I couldn't think of anything better.

"Yeah," she said. "Because I don't have to work."

"Shall we go to a club?"

"Oh, yeah!"

"Cool!"

Jan set to work now with some white varnish, her tongue pressed against the side of her cheek as she carefully created a design.

"Kayla's got loads of toys and stuff, hasn't she?" I said.

"Yeah," Jan said absently, "but some of them are mine."

"Really?"

"Mango the bear is," she said, pointing to the big polar bear thing. "And them dolls. I like dolls. I collect them. And I sleep with Ewan – that dog over there." I saw a tatty old dog with one eye missing.

"That's nice," I said, not knowing what else to say. "How long have you had him?"

"Since I was a kid," she said.

"Was he a present?" I asked, interested in Jan's life. She carried on painting, talking.

"I won him in a raffle at primary school."

"So when you left home, you took him with you?"

"Yeah. I ran away from home."

"Did you?" I tried not to sound too curious, didn't want to break the spell.

"Yeah. I couldn't stand it there. There was no money or nothing, and my mum giving me grief, shouting all the time. And she hit me all the time, she said it was the only way to control me. But I reckon she wasn't my mother, right? I had clues, like, I didn't look like her, not at all. Then she got this boyfriend who gave me the creeps and kept ordering me around. Made me do the housework, like all of it. I was like a slave. Angie, do this! Angie, do that! Yeah, and he used to bawl at all of us. It was horrible. I had to have free dinners at school, we were so poor. That pissed me off. My mates had stuff, clothes and that. I didn't. I wouldn't have run away if my mum didn't hate me, though. But she did. She really hated me. I could see it in her eyes. I thought maybe if I ran away I could find my real mother, maybe my dad too. But mostly I thought if I could run away it would be better than this. No one breathing down my neck. I could be free to do whatever I wanted.

"So I did run away. It was dead easy. One morning I went to school with some extra clothes and that, and Ewan, and then just didn't go home. I found my way to town. It was just brilliant, being all by myself, not having to worry about anyone else. I felt like I could do anything. I mean, I was mad, I was still in my school uniform. I changed in the toilet, threw my uniform in a bin. I was like full of energy, having an adventure. I just kept walking. When I got tired I found a telephone box and went in there. I settled down to sleep hugging Ewan. Then when it got light, when I woke up, my school bag had gone. Someone nicked it. But it was the morning and I had Ewan and some money still in my pocket. Like, I'd helped myself before I left.

"My main worry now was that they might start looking for me. Yeah. But Ali and Jono said to ring a number and say I was all right, then they would be off my back. So I did. I slept in the multi-storey car park with them but then the security guards, real bastards, threw us out. There wasn't anywhere to wash or anything. And then my money went. It was scary, living on the streets. You got to be careful, have your wits about you. Watch out. Sally was really good to me. She said I could kip here."

"So do you have a job now?" I asked.

"Yeah," she said. "Bar work. Some nights."

"Where? Which pub? I'll come in and see you."

"Different pubs," she said. "There's some red too. I'll use that."

I was trying to make sense of what Jan had told me. Obviously she was earning money illegally, maybe claiming dole and getting wages too. Which explained why she might be working under different names, and why those older blokes recognised her as Mary. Everything was falling into place now. I was sorry that she'd had such a bad childhood, and I guessed there were worse things that she hadn't told me. And why did she call herself Angie? But that was the past. She was brave to leave home. Braver than me. Because maybe it was about time for me to think of leaving home.

She'd painted my toes like targets. Black background, white concentric circles and a spot of red in the centre. I was really pleased with them. I felt a bit scared of doing hers as I wasn't very artistic – I was bound to make a mess of them.

"Your turn now," I said.

"Yeah, wait," she said. "I want to show you something." She reached over for her bag, opened her purse, got out a ring. It was scalloped silver. I admired it. I was beginning to understand why Jan was so into her possessions. If she'd left home, they were all she had. It wasn't that she was showing off – her watch, this ring were significant to her.

"And look," she went on. "I got my own phone now. But I got to get a Sim card for it. You can get them from newsagents." She showed me the phone. It was a silver Motorola Wings. My stomach did a somersault.

"Can I see it?" I asked. She handed it to me. There, on the back, were Melissa's initials. I'd seen them before. When Melissa had had them done she made sure everyone knew about it. I gave Jan back the phone.

"Where did you get this?" I asked her, dead neutral.

"Found it," she said. Her tone had changed. She acted hurt, as if I was accusing her of something. Suddenly she seemed very young, like a kid, not like my age at all.

"Where did you find it?" I asked.

"Under a bush," she said. "What else do you want to know?" Those were her words, but they were dead sarcastic. She meant, ask me another question and you can get out. It was the first test of our friendship. I decided to back off.

"It was just that I'd always wanted one of these," I said. "They're cool." Jan shot me a look, then began to relax.

"Yeah. They are." She grinned at me. "When I can get it to work, we can text each other, like you and Taz do."

I went a bit quiet then. Had Jan told me the truth? Did she just *find* the phone? Maybe the criminals who smashed Melissa's car window flung the phone away. It was more likely than Jan being one of the criminals. I knew she shoplifted, but grabbing a handbag like that was different. It was more of a male crime. Then I thought about the blokes she kept mentioning, Ali and Jono. Had they been the criminals? Had they given her the phone?

It didn't matter. What mattered more was what I should do now. I knew I really ought to explain to Jan that I knew who the phone really belonged to, and we ought to return it. Hey – Melissa might even give a reward! I tried to imagine myself talking Jan into doing this. But it all seemed wrong. It felt like I would be betraying Jan, forcing the values of my world on to hers. And Melissa already had another phone. This one was effectively worthless. It was so middle class, giving things back to whom they belong. The whole ownership thing. What the hell, let her keep Melissa's phone.

At that moment I realised I'd crossed over. What's the phrase? I compounded a felony. I was letting Jan hang on to stolen property. I was part of the crime. A criminal, too.

But I was left feeling uneasy. I was unsure of my decision, I had to keep going back in my mind and testing it. And there was something about Jan's reaction when I had confronted her that troubled me. It was how she came over so defensive, so young. How old was she exactly? I'd never asked her, just assumed, because she was the same height as me, that we were the same age. But now I wondered. Because I wouldn't need to *run* away from home, I could just leave home. I could get social security money. But if Jan was under sixteen, she couldn't.

I looked at her again. Tried to guess her age. Fifteen? Fourteen? Even younger? It was possible.

But then, what does age matter? Let's not get ageist here. I mean, you must be at least forty – I don't mean to be rude, only it's hard to tell with your shaved head. And the United shirt. You're not a dad, are you, but you help with Linda's kids, I know. I bet you're like their dad. Do they wake you up in the morning? I suppose, if you're a parent, that must be the best thing, seeing your kids all sleepy in the morning, trying to clamber into your bed. Yeah. I did that once. It's hard to believe. I'm a different person entirely now. On my own. Like Jan.

To Taz (7)

Check this out. It's a verse of a poem.

> Like one, that on a lonesome road
> Doth walk in fear and dread,
> And having once looked round, walks on,
> And turns no more his head;
> Because he knows a frightful fiend
> Doth close behind him tread.

I found that quoted in *Frankenstein,* the book by Mary Shelley. I was bored, I started reading. I thought *Frankenstein* was going to be like the film, Boris Karloff with the bolt through his head, but it wasn't. It was much better than the film. Frankenstein is actually the guy who makes the monster. Only when he makes it, he realises he's made a huge mistake. And this verse is like how he feels. The monster is always following him. A Frightful Fiend. And the monster is getting closer. And results day was getting closer. The poem the verse comes from is called *The Ancient Mariner.* I read the rest of it. It says:

And I had done a hellish thing,
And it would work 'em woe:

Because my parents really thought everything was all right. That I had sat my exams, that I would get all As as usual, and everything would be OK. So on August 18th all hell would be let loose. People I knew were stressing about results but no one had the reasons to stress that I did.

It was hard to imagine what my parents would do. They might be angry, but worse, there would be this big inquisition. More meetings at school, decisions. So I was drinking to get to sleep, then waking at four in the morning, pulse racing, heart thumping. You knew all that, because I told you. You said to me maybe I ought to speak to my parents beforehand. I kept putting it off. I said to you, OK, so you tell your parents you think you're gay. You said, not yet. Quite, I said.

And then Spence asked you to go away with him on the trip to Amsterdam. I know you also had to lie to your parents about who you were going with. That's where you are now, Taz. So you don't know anything about what happened afterwards.

The only person I could talk to was Jan. She was great. She didn't seem to think exams mattered. When I was with her we lived for the moment. Sometimes she had money and we went clubbing. She knew where to get fake IDs. Sally didn't seem to mind me coming round, though she never spoke to me much. What Jan and I liked doing was making plans. She had all these crazy ideas, about going to America, getting a flat in New York. I think she'd seen too much *Friends*. I'd scale down the plans a bit, and said then we could get a flat together here. She said she'd like that, the baby was getting her down. So we planned it all out. How I would leave home and we'd take a train to another town and set up there. I never meant to do that. It was pure fantasy. The truth was, I was paralysed with fear. I was incapable of taking any action. I wanted to. I wanted to do something dramatic, something that mattered. Something that would make my messed-up exam papers pale into insignificance. But what? It was easier to have fun, live for the moment, be Jan's mate, be wild and free.

Then my mum found out about my drinking. I suppose she was bound to, in the end. I had this system for getting rid of cans now. I'd keep them in a plastic bag in my room, then late at night – the night before the men came to empty the wheelie bin – I'd put them in, rearranging the rubbish so they were out of sight.

That morning I stayed in bed until I heard the bins emptied then wandered downstairs for coffee, thinking my mother had gone to work by then. Dad I knew was in London. But there was Mum, sitting in the kitchen with my plastic bag full of empties on the breakfast bar. The funny thing was I wanted to laugh. I guess it was hysteria. She was horribly matter of fact.

"I was looking for the receipt for the trousers I bought from Debenhams," she said. "The ones I want to exchange. I decided I must have thrown it away – a reflex action. I thought I'd look through the rubbish this morning and found this."

"Gross," I remarked, went over to the kettle.

"How did all these cans get here?"

"Maybe someone from the street threw them in?"

"Along with the empty bottle of vodka Dad brought back from Germany?"

I went cold.

"Explain, Catherine."

Damn. My mind wasn't properly engaged. I hesitated too long.

"*Now* I understand," she said, her voice nervous and exultant all at once. "Why you haven't been working, your mood swings. My God, I'd thought of drugs, but it never crossed my mind that you'd be drinking *beer*! Just tell me, exactly how much have you been drinking?"

"Not that much," I said, my back towards her.

"The truth, Catherine."

"I don't really know."

I think I would have preferred it had she ranted, called me an alcoholic, so then I would have had the right to be angry. Instead each of us was careful not to put a foot wrong, aware that one false step and we would fall into a pit.

"I'd prefer you to tell me," she said.

"I'd prefer not to," I replied.

"So you have got something to hide."

"I don't see why it's your business."

"You're not eighteen yet."

"It's still none of your business."

"Catherine?" Her voice was sharp with threat. This was awful. I poured out water from the kettle into my mug, watched it turn dark brown with dissolving coffee powder.

"When your father gets home from London tonight we'll all talk about this together. I have to get to work now."

And that was it. She collected her things and went. I didn't turn to look at her. She left the cans on the table. I remembered something Jan had said, about how she believed her mother hated her. At the time I thought, no mother can hate her child, but now I knew different. I felt nothing but contempt from my mother. Perhaps she'd have preferred it if I snorted coke, did something acceptably shocking, that rich people did. But I drank. Beer, mainly.

Now what? The idea of having to wait all day until a showdown was unbearable. It was her way of torturing me. It was the old threat, *wait until your father gets home.*

She chose the timing of the showdown, so that she had control. I was powerless. I drank my coffee, felt sick. Showered, came down, watched TV. I was just pretending everything was normal.

Then I thought, this is stupid, so I got my things and went out. It was a bit dull, threatening rain. I didn't have anywhere special to go, so I headed into town. I thought it might take me out of myself. But it didn't. There was nothing new in any of the stores, just the remnants of the sales. It was while I was wandering around New Look in the middle of the afternoon that I realised I needn't go home at all.

I stood still, rooted to the spot. It would teach them a lesson. It would also defer a confrontation. It would also be making a statement. It would be my way of saying how bad I felt. Then they would feel sorry for me. I know all this reads really childishly, but I was thinking with my emotions. I was scared and feeling sorry for myself. But I also felt as if I wanted to prove my independence. To show them I had my own life. That they really didn't have any control over me at all.

What I would do was just stay out. I could easily spend the rest of the afternoon in town, then maybe go round to Jan's. I'd leave a message on the answerphone telling Mum and Dad not to worry. Then I'd come in late. *I* would choose the time of our confrontation. They would have to wait for me. I would be making a statement, a statement I had a perfect right to make. If I wanted to. Because my other choice would be never to go home. Jan made that choice, and she was surviving. Who's to say that I couldn't?

I cheered up then. I left the shop and crossed over to McDonald's and had a burger. I wondered what to do with the rest of my time. I was a bit reluctant to go over to Jan's too early because sometimes Sally could be a bit off with me – after all, it was her house. I decided to wait until the evening so that Jan and I could go straight out. Then I had a brilliant idea – I'd go and see a film.

It was weird, going by myself. Weirder still entering a cinema in the middle of the day. I got a ticket, bought myself some popcorn, and chose a romantic comedy. It was nice just sitting there in an almost empty cinema, like it was your own private screen. There were a few other couples but no one on their own like me. I wasn't fussed. I settled down to watch the film. I just wanted to escape.

The film was all right, nothing special. A lot of American people doing crazy things, mad things. I thought how you could play the same events – misunderstandings, hating someone while secretly fancying them – as if they were tragedy. Life was life, and depending how you looked at it, it was either funny or dreadful. I could imagine this sitcom about a girl who deliberately fails her exams, fancies a boy who turns out to be almost gay, whose parents discover her alcohol stash. Hilarious.

If I spoke to my parents that night I thought I might explain about the exams, get it over and done with. If they were in listening mode, that was. The trouble with my parents is that you felt they always had their own agenda. I wondered if I was the only person who loved their parents but didn't like them much. Maybe it would be different when I was older. Maybe not.

The film ended. My mouth was sticky with popcorn. I would have bought some Coke in the foyer but they only sold huge containers of the stuff. I checked my watch and saw it was after six. I thought I'd go and have a real drink, so I went in a nearby pub and ordered myself half a lager. It was a little seedy in there, and everyone else in the pub were saddos. A bloke with greasy hair and black-framed glasses reading the evening newspaper. Two red-faced boys around my age, puffed, drunk faces. An old chap looking terminally depressed. And me. The place was doing my head in. I drank up my beer and went to call in at Jan's.

What I reckoned was, my dad would get home around seven. They'd wonder where I was. Let them wonder. Let them wonder maybe till nine or ten. Then I could ring again, and either tell them I was on my way, or that I was taking a break. It was a terrifying, exhilarating thought. Leaving home felt like one of those rollercoaster rides where you face a vertical drop. It could be the worst experience of your life, or the best. Did I have the courage to find out?

Maybe later – not now. I took the bus to Maple Street, walked quickly up to Jan's house. Knocked. Sally opened the door and I asked for Jan.

"Sorry," she said. "She's out."

I hadn't expected that.

"When will she be back?"

Sally shrugged, gave me the impression she didn't want to tell me. I didn't like that.

"Where has she gone?" I asked.

I saw Sally deliberate. I didn't know what she was deliberating about. I do now.

She said, "She's up the Old Manchester Road."

Old Manchester Road? There was nothing there except for a tatty industrial estate, derelict warehouses and a string of car showrooms.

"Go and see if you can find her," Sally said, and shut the door in my face.

To Taz (8)

It all felt crazy, getting on the bus to the Old Manchester Road, knowing my mother was at home by now expecting my dad and wondering where I was. There wasn't any sense in it. Even though I'd made all this happen, I still felt as if it hadn't been my choice. Then I switched my thoughts off. I was looking for Jan.

It was late evening but not yet dark when I got off the bus outside the Premier Fashions wholesale outlet. I glanced around. There was absolutely no one in sight. There was no reason for anyone to be in the area. During the day people worked in the warehouses or visited the car showrooms I'd just been past, but now it was a no-man's land. No people, no animals, no trees, just scraps of waste ground with placards saying which property company had acquired them. Although I'd been past the area loads of times, I'd never noticed it before, just somewhere between town and the suburbs.

Still, I reckoned if Sally had sent me here without further directions I should be able to find Jan. Maybe there was a pub up here she served in. I didn't really know. I started walking up the road, traffic rushing past me. Maybe there would be a clue or something.

I didn't need a clue. I saw Jan. She was standing on the corner by a boarded-up house. I knew it was her. Her long hair was unmistakable, and she was wearing boots – boots I'd not seen before, and that silly very short skirt I remembered from the first time we met in the Gardens. I quickened my pace. I wondered what she was doing there? Maybe visiting her old family?

Then a car drew to a halt by her, someone who was lost and asking for directions, I reckoned. And Jan got in, in the passenger seat, which was a pretty stupid thing to do. I ran towards her. You'd have thought she'd have realised that was dangerous. By the time I was approaching the car it was too late. They had driven off. My chest was hurting from the exercise, and I was worried. Why did she go off like that? Maybe she knew whoever it was. I hoped so.

Once again I didn't know what to do with myself. I was feeling anxious now. This wasn't a good area. I had half a mind to go back to town and get a bus home. In fact a bus passed me on the other side of the road going somewhere or other. It looked inviting. Only I was reluctant to give up on Jan, and curious as to why she got into that car. It was an old Ford Escort. I would have tried to remember the number plate if I'd had enough presence of mind.

I decided then she wouldn't have got into a car with a complete stranger, even to show them the way. It would have been a stupid thing to do. Standing on that street corner like that someone could have easily mistaken her for a prostitute.

My mind froze.

No – Jan couldn't be! Not a prostitute! That was silly. Like, she never even seemed very interested in blokes when we went out. She didn't live with a pimp, a slimy bloke who she gave her earnings to. She was pretty, she didn't need to, and anyway – I admitted this to myself now – she was only about thirteen.

I wanted to persuade myself I was wrong, but I couldn't. I was thinking in stereotypes. I realised I knew nothing about prostitutes. The truth was, Jan had never told me exactly how she supported herself. There was shoplifting, sure, but other times she had money with her, more money than you could ever get from shoplifting.

If this was true – and I thought I was disgusting for even imagining it – then I had to save her. There was no way I was going to leave. I was staying here until Jan got back. If she got back.

I don't know how long I waited because time stood still. I didn't want to think. I just focused on the traffic, on a couple I saw in the distance who walked up the Old Manchester Road and down a side road to somewhere or other. I stared at the warehouse signs. Waited. Had to see Jan. Would have waited all night if needs be.

But I didn't have to. The same car dropped her off fairly near where I was standing. There was hardly any doubt now. I called her name as I ran towards her.

"Jan!"

She jerked round, saw me. She began to run too, away from me. I increased my pace, commanding her to stop. She ran like the wind. I didn't call after her – I saved my breath for the pursuit. She turned down a side street – I followed. At the end I saw there were boards – someone was building there. Jan knew she was cornered. She stopped for just one moment. That gave me time to catch up with her. I grabbed her by the shoulders. She jerked away.

"Jan, please!"

"What are you doing here?" she asked angrily.

"Sally told me. She said I'd find you here."

"She's a cow. I know her problem. She's jealous. She's jealous of you being my mate. She wants to spoil it for me."

I wondered then about Sally and Jan's relationship. But only for a moment. The main thing was to save Jan. I had to stop her doing what she was doing. I knew better than to preach at her. That was why I turned the conversation to me and my needs. I thought it would defuse the situation.

"Look, Jan. I wanted to find you because I'm having hassle off my parents. I was, like, thinking about leaving them."

She looked at me oddly.

"My mum discovered how much I'd been drinking. So I walked out. I haven't decided what to do yet, but I wanted to find you. Because you're my best mate," I added.

Her face softened. "Am I?"

"Come here." We went to sit on a nearby wall. I waited while she lit a cigarette and inhaled it greedily. I told her briefly about my day. She relaxed; our relationship began to return to normal. Then little by little I turned the conversation to her. I wanted to get her to talk. I asked her little prompting questions, and bit by bit it all came out. Let me tell you what she told me.

She said, she never meant to become a prostitute. She wasn't one, really. It was only what she did to get money. The money was the problem. She said she couldn't get dole money, she was too young. She couldn't get a proper job. She couldn't even sell The Big Issue. But the kids she was hanging round with after she first ran away told her she could earn twenty, maybe thirty quid for a hand job. At first she was totally disgusted but then she gave the idea some headspace. Yeah, the idea was rank. But then she thought, anyone does anything for enough money. Everyone has their price. People kill for money, they risk their reputations, don't they, Taz? Just for money. What Jan did wasn't that bad.

She said these friends of hers told her where to go. But she was a bit grossed-out by the idea. She came into the Gardens instead to buy some time. That was the night I first met her. The vodka sorted her, she said. She was out of her head after it. She went round the back of a furniture warehouse, a loading bay. There were condoms, needles on the floor. His breath stunk. It was foul, disgusting. She tried to fill her head with other stuff, like all those rap lyrics. It sort of worked, she said, because it didn't seem real what she was doing. It was like someone else was jerking him off. But still she was sick afterwards. She was just glad she didn't throw up all over the punter. Or maybe she should've done – he deserved it, the pervert. But he gave her twenty quid.

She'd shacked up with Sally at that time. She gave Sally some rent so it meant she had somewhere to stay. And she had money to spend on herself. The second time it was easier. She knew to get drunk first. And it made her feel good, to earn money off those stinky old men. And you had to be careful, you had to have your own patch. But Sally arranged that with the other women. Sally was on the game too. Jan said the other women were great, had a sense of humour, looked after her, told her where to get stuff. On the streets she was Mary. When she was a little girl, a kid, she was Angie.

Then she thought she might as well do full sex, like, what's the difference? The money's better – the night of George's party she was given fifty quid by a punter. Some nights she might get two punters – it adds up. She said she knows what people think about what she does, but she's supporting herself. It's her body, and she can do what she wants with it. She's had to watch out for the police, duck and dive, but once this copper came up to her, and she was about to run, but he only wanted a hand job.

As we talked, she was chain smoking. What I couldn't get over was that she was so matter of fact. You know, Taz, everything else that had happened to me, I was able to accept. I was able to adjust my vision. But not now. I couldn't accept this. I'd reached my limits. I couldn't bear to think of what men did to Jan. I had to do something.

"Don't you think these men are exploiting you?" I suggested.

She looked blank. "Whatever," she said.

I realised she hadn't understood the word. "They're using you," I explained.

"They pay," she said. "I need the money."

"If I gave you some money…" I calculated rapidly – I had five hundred pounds in my savings account – "… say, five hundred pounds, would you give this up?"

"Have you got five hundred quid with you?"

"Not with me. But I can get it."

"Oh." She stubbed out her cigarette. "Yeah, well, I'm not doing this for ever anyway. I'm moving on soon. I got enough to rent a flat. Somewhere else. I'll get a real job then, working in a shop. I'll get a discount off the clothes."

"Are you old enough to work in a shop?"

"Yeah, well, a girl in my class at school did a paper round. And helped out in the shop in the evenings."

"What year were you in at school?"

"Year Eight."

I was right. She was only thirteen, possibly even twelve. I felt sick, cold. She was Jan, my Jan, sitting next to me, but I didn't know her at all. Not at all. I was out of my depth. Utterly helpless. I wanted my mum and dad then, my teacher, anyone.

"Yeah," she said. "I'll get a job. And buy lottery tickets. And then I'll settle down and get married and have those four kids, Adam, Zak, Bella and Rosy. Maybe I'll paint. I could open my own nail salon. We could go now, Cat. You and me. Go to a new town and open a beauty salon."

"Yeah. If you went back to school you could get some qualifications."

"I'm not going back to school. No way."

"But isn't school better than what you're doing?"

She was silent. I held my breath.

"No," she said, after a while. "No. Teachers dissing you and this girl held my head down the toilets. I never had no money. No. This is all right for now. I'm earning money, aren't I? I'm looking after myself. It can be pretty crappy, but like, what's perfect? And it's not for ever."

She took two twenty-pound notes out of her jacket pocket and looked at them, hoping I would notice and be impressed. She put them back.

"Maybe you wouldn't have to go back to school," I continued. "They could find you a foster home or something."

"I'm not going into effing care. I've heard about what happens."

"Do you have a relation? An aunt or someone who could look after you till you're old enough to leave home properly?"

"Just lay off, will you?"

I felt stupid, stupid and young. Much younger than Jan. Who had left home, and was looking after herself as well as she knew how. Who'd made a choice and was sticking to it. But I'd chosen to help her. I couldn't lay off, like she said. I had to keep going.

"Spend the night with me! Come back to my house. I'll lend you some of my clothes. We're the same size."

She turned and looked at me. It was like she was in a different place, a different country. I realised we had nothing in common at all.

"We can still be best mates," I said.

"Yeah, whatever."

She got up, walked down the street. I followed her.

"Shall we go for a drink?"

"No," she said. "I owe Sally. And I lost my Walkman. I want to buy another one. So, beat it, because I got to work."

We reached the end of the street.

"Bye," I said.

She didn't even say goodbye.

I just walked on, back to town, away from her. All she had told me went round and round my head, fixing itself in my memory. In the end it felt as if it had all happened to me, all those disgusting, vile things. I felt sick. I remembered Jan's voice, the way she talked in bursts between inhaling. How her mouth moved faster than the words that came out. The way she emphasised certain words. Her tone: proud, defensive, bitter.

I felt more of a failure than ever. I couldn't even rescue her. I was good for nothing. Tears stung my eyes, but I wouldn't give in to self-pity. That isn't my style. I was more shocked and angry. Angry with myself for being so selfish, just seeing Jan as someone who fitted into my life and blinding myself to the fact that her problems were so much bigger than mine. Angry, too, at all the people out there who preyed on girls like Jan.

I didn't know where I was walking to. It hardly seemed to matter whether I went home or not. My predicament paled into insignificance against Jan's. I could only think of her. I wondered what I'd meant to her. Maybe I was just part of her fantasy world and helped her to believe she was leading a normal, teenage life. Maybe she was part of my fantasy world, too, making me think I was wild and free and independent, when I wasn't. We both peddled dangerous illusions to each other. We were better apart.

It was dark now. I thought I ought not to be walking alone and decided to get a bus back into town. After that, I didn't know. I saw a bus shelter ahead of me but its one pane of glass had been shattered into green crystal shards which lay in a heap nearby. Avoiding the glass and the litter scattered in the shelter, I stood a good few yards away, my eyes fixed in the distance, watching for a bus, hoping I wouldn't have to wait too long.

And then I saw a car. A Ford Escort. It was driving slowly, given that the road was almost empty. It came to a halt by me. My heart beat faster. There was no doubt in my mind that this was the same car that Jan had got into.

I wasn't scared, Taz. I was furious. And here was my chance to stand up for Jan, even if she would never find out.

A man, shaven-headed, slitty-eyed, smelling of fag-ends and in last season's football shirt, wound down his window and asked me if I wanted a lift.

I reached over and with all the force I could muster I slapped him round the face.

To Dave (S)

You're really solid, Dave. You must be, because you hardly flinched. You swore a bit, but then said, "So what's that all about, then?"

"Do I have to explain?" I shouted.

"Yeah," you said.

So I did. "Because you're filthy and exploitative. Because you're so dysfunctional that you can't get any decent woman to go to bed with you so you have to cruise round in this old wreck looking for girls who are young enough to be your daughters. You're just utterly pathetic. I wouldn't even waste my spit on you. You think just because you pay the kids you've squared up. But what if she was your own daughter? Have you thought of that? Your generation is so effing selfish, that's what it is. You all mouth off about doing things for kids, educating them, buying things for them, but the truth is you only want what *you* want. You call it a business transaction to mask the fact you're meeting your perverted needs. You're irresponsible. You make kids like Jan do things and don't think about it from their point of view. You think you're such a tough guy just because of your beer gut and your motor but you're worse than an animal. You've got a brain and you don't use it. Violence is the only bloody language you understand."

And that was when I started kicking your car, Dave. It was such a relief as my foot hit the metal, the dull thuds, the rocking of the car. I didn't care that my foot was red with pain. I needed to express what I felt.

"Stop it," you said to me. "You'll wake the kids up."

Then I heard a long, sleepy wail from the back of the car. It puzzled me. You turned round to the back and my eyes followed yours. I saw a plump, angry, bleary-eyed toddler and a smaller baby who was still slumped over in sleep. For a moment I couldn't take it in. I'd never heard of a kerb-crawler with his kids in the back. I watched you wriggle round and fish for a dummy that had fallen by the side of the baby seat. You gave it to the toddler who greedily stuck it in its mouth and stared at me as if I was from Outer Space.

"I think you've made a mistake," you said to me. "I asked you if you wanted a lift because I don't think girls like you should be hanging around here at this time of night."

Slowly I realised you were telling the truth. Even then it occurred to me that there was something stupendously funny about the whole thing. You'd only wanted to help and I'd vented all my rage on you. I reddened with humiliation and would have walked away but you carried on talking.

"These kids in the back are Linda's," you said. "Linda's my sister. I've had them for the day while she was out with her fella. I'm taking them back now. Can I drop you somewhere?"

It was the kindness in the tone of your voice. You made me see myself as you saw me, a young girl, scared and lonely, out by herself, in need of protection. And so I began to feel sorry for myself. And you know what happens when people feel sorry for themselves – they cry. All the confusion and fear of the last few weeks finally found expression. I sobbed and sobbed. You twisted round again to hunt around in a bag full of baby things and handed me a tissue with Winnie the Pooh on it. I blew my nose loudly.

You got out of the car now, keeping your distance from me.

"What's your name?" you asked.

"Catherine," I said. "Catherine Holmes."

"Do you live round here?"

"No." I mentioned the suburb I lived in.

"I'll take you there if you like," you said.

I shook my head vehemently. I still didn't know whether I wanted to go home. Then you introduced yourself. You said you weren't in a hurry. You suggested I go and sit in the bus shelter and you'd sit with me until I felt better. You could keep an eye on the kids from there.

I did what you said. There was something about the way you didn't foist your help on me that made me want to accept it. I reckoned I was safe sitting there with traffic whizzing past. I wasn't exactly alone with you. I trusted you, but on the other hand I'd been brought up not to talk to strangers and you were a stranger.

"Who's Jan?" you asked.

And I explained. There was no need to hold back because you could have guessed anyway. I told my story in a jumble. That I'd discovered Jan was a prostitute. That I'd made friends with her because I thought she was lonely like me. I told you about Taz, who was so different from me. And how I'd started drinking. How I'd screwed up my exams, and couldn't see the point of working any more. That I felt robbed of freedom in my life, and how everyone thought they knew what was best for me. That I'd stopped connecting with anyone or anything. It was strange sitting there and trying to be coherent, telling the story of my life to someone I'd never met before. But doing that began to create a sense of order, of inevitability.

When I finished you were quiet for a bit. Then you asked, did I mind if you smoked. I shook my head. You lit up a Player's.

"It seems a shame, if you've got the brains, not to use them," you said.

"But what if I don't want to?"

"It's your choice," you said.

You made it sound so simple but it wasn't. I was beginning to see how one choice led to another. Jan chose to run away from home and then discovered that the only choice that lay open to her was to support herself by prostitution. A rational choice, but a potentially deadly one. Taz couldn't choose to be straight or gay. Taz's mum regretted her choice. How would I know if I was choosing right or not when everyone around me was screwing up?

"I've failed all my exams," I said.

"You can take them again." I knew that was true.

"But then what?" I argued. "More exams, more pressure."

"What do you want to do?" you asked. "Like, for a career?"

It was the old question, and I bridled. What did I want to be when I grew up? Only there was something this time that made me pause. You had said, what do you want to *do*? That sounded different. What did I want to *do*?

"Help girls like Jan, I suppose. I don't know how, though."

"You'd probably need qualifications," you said.

I nodded. But my mind was elsewhere, with Jan. I felt rotten, just leaving her like that. I needed to find her again. I couldn't do that alone. The best thing would be to go home and ask my parents for help. I could take the humiliation involved. I couldn't pretend it would be easy. I was still scared of their reaction but knew I could never, and would never want to, go back to being the good, obedient Catherine they loved. I would have to go home on my own terms. Those terms would have to include telling the truth, as far as it was ever possible to tell the truth.

Stray thoughts played around in my mind. They needn't pay for me to retake my ASs. I could go to the college. Perhaps a sixth-form college would suit me better. I could look into a vocational course. I had to be honest about the amount of pressure I could take. My parents would have to accept that, and I would have to take on board that it wouldn't be easy for them, either, to accept that I was fundamentally different from them. We all have our dreams and illusions: Jan, me, even my parents.

I'd made a mess and it was up to me to clear it up. Just like it was brave of Jan to run away and I felt no pity for her, only a determination to give her something better, I realised it would be brave of me to go home. Perhaps, Dave, it was your common sense infecting me, I don't know. Then you got up and went to check the kids. I watched you stick your head through the window and felt more embarrassed than ever at the way I'd misjudged you. You turned round then and said that you'd better get the kids back to Linda else she'd be fretting. You asked me again if I wanted a lift.

The odd thing was, I hesitated. I hope you weren't hurt by that. It was then the police car drew up, its blue lights flashing. Two young constables got out, a man and woman.

"What's going on here?" the policeman asked you. I noticed the cosh on his belt and his walkie-talkie radio. I saw the policewoman eyeing me. I realised things looked worse for you than they did for me so I stepped in to explain.

"It's all right," I said. "I was lost, and he stopped to help me. His name's Dave. He's been looking after his sister's kids. I was on my way home. I was a bit upset, that was why he stopped."

You nodded. "So you're going home now?" you asked.

"Yeah," I said.

The smile you gave me made me certain I was doing the right thing.

The policewoman asked where I lived and I told her. They offered to drive me there. I accepted, rather relishing the idea of arriving home under police escort. I hadn't quite given up wanting to shock my parents.

I shook your hand, Dave, and asked for your name and address so I could write and thank you.

"Let me know how you get on," you said.

"I will."

"It might do you good to write it all down," you added.

I told you I'd do that. You got into your car then and drove off. I noticed one of your rear lights wasn't working, and so did the copper, but he didn't say anything. I got into the back of the patrol car and realised I'd almost reached the end of my journey.

But if I was going to write it all down, where would I start? And who would it be for? Because the problem with any story is that you tell it differently depending on who you think is reading it. I can't write only for me, in the same way that I can't live my life only for me. Other people matter. So I would have to think of the other people in my story too, and tell them what it looked like from where I was standing.

If I tried to connect with them, maybe they could connect with me.